'You're very ...
Dr Buchanan

'I. . .' Words w...
thank you.'

'Don't thank me.' His eyes narrowed with laughter. 'There's another reason you'd best recover fast. It's against all medical ethics to proposition a patient, and if you knew just how beautiful you are. . .' His fingers traced the contours of her face. 'Well, enough for now,' he added softly. 'Just recover fast.'

Kids. . .one of life's joys, one of life's treasures.

Kisses. . .of warmth, kisses of passion, kisses from mothers and kisses from lovers.

In *Kids & Kisses*. . .every story has it all.

Marion Lennox has had a variety of careers—medical receptionist, computer programmer and teacher. Married, with two young children, she now lives in rural Victoria, Australia. Her wish for an occupation which would allow her to remain at home with her children and her dog led her to begin writing, and she has now published a number of medical romances.

Recent titles by the same author:
DOCTOR'S HONOUR
PRACTICE MAKES MARRIAGE
STORM HAVEN
ONE CARING HEART

DANGEROUS
PHYSICIAN

BY
MARION LENNOX

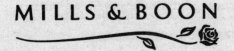

MILLS & BOON

MILLS & BOON, the Rose Device and
LOVE ON CALL *are trademarks of the publisher.*
Harlequin Mills & Boon Limited,
Eton House, 18-24 Paradise Road, Richmond, Surrey TW9 1SR
This edition published by arrangement with Harlequin Enterprises B.V.

© Marion Lennox 1995

ISBN 0 263 79336 2

Set in Times 10 on 11 pt. by
Rowland Phototypesetting Limited
Bury St Edmunds, Suffolk

03-9509-48599

Made and printed in Great Britain
Cover illustration by Ruth Swain

CHAPTER ONE

GINA BUCHANAN was a very careful doctor. Impulsive acts were for children—she'd decided that years ago. So. . .

So she shouldn't stop. It was dark and Wayne was waiting, but the sign said View Point and the distant lights beneath the mountain were beautiful. The temptation was too great. For once Gina acted on impulse.

Gundowring lay below as a shimmering cluster of light. The rising moon lit a silver trail across the ocean to join the dark waters of the river-mouth, and while she watched a fishing-boat moved slowly into harbour. Magic. . .

Gina breathed the warm night air of Australian summer and felt good for the first time since she'd agreed to marry Wayne.

'It is the right thing,' she whispered. 'I can be happy here. Secure. . .' Then she frowned. She turned back from the safety rail as the silence disappeared in a muted roar.

By the time she reached her car, the roar was no longer muted. Twenty. . . No, thirty or more motor-bikes coming straight up the mountain.

They turned off the road into the look-out. . .

It was OK. They were just bikers stopping for a look—just like her. It had to be OK.

It wasn't.

By the time Gina had the engine going she was surrounded by a sea of bikes. There was nowhere she could go, and the leader—a man on a huge, mud-caked machine—was dismounting and strolling over to yank open her door.

'Well, well,' he drawled, and his voice was slurred with alcohol. 'Someone else admiring the view.'

'Please. . .' Gina had difficulty getting the word out. 'Please, let me close my door. I'm just leaving.'

'Leaving? Now, is that polite? We've only just arrived—and we'd love some company.'

Silence. The other bikers were gradually cutting their motors as they strained to hear.

'I'm not. . .I need to go. Can you let me go, please?'

He looked down at her for a long, long moment. The man was big, heavy-jowled and unshaven. His leathers were covered in obscenities, greasy hair hung lankly from under his helmet and something tucked inside his jacket moved. A snout appeared, and Gina stared in horror as a pit bull-terrier stuck its face out from the opening at the neck of his jacket. Teeth bared in a snarl. Like dog, like owner, she thought fleetingly. The resemblance was horrible.

'Now, that's no way to talk to a lady,' he told the dog. The man shoved the dog's snout back. With a swift movement his hand came down, and Gina's slight body was yanked roughly from the car. 'Especially one as pretty as this. What's your name, sweetheart?'

'Gina—Dr Buchanan. . .' Gina strove desperately for calm—for authority. 'I'm—I'm expected down at the hospital.

'Doctor. . .' The man's eyes roved over Gina's slim body. She was wearing a soft white blouse, tight jeans and sandals, and her mass of white-blonde hair was tumbling free. Gina's blue eyes were huge in her white face. 'You don't look like any doctor I ever saw.'

'I am. . .'

He grinned. 'Well, I believe you, lady.' His hand didn't lessen its grip—in fact it tightened. 'A doctor.' His free hand came up to tilt her chin. 'I've never made it with a doctor.'

There was a nervous titter around them. Thirty spectators. . .

'You touch me and I'll have you in gaol so fast——' Somehow Gina managed to say the words, but the voice she heard didn't sound like her own. Then she gave a cry of pain as he put a hand in her hair and wrenched her backwards. As she lost her footing he jerked her arm and kept dragging.

'Gaol? Yeah? You and whose army?'

She shouldn't have said it. The man was drunk and her threat was a red rag to a bull. He was swearing savagely, his hand twisting in her hair as he hauled her through the mass of riders towards the edge of the clearing.

There was nothing she could do. The man was so strong. . . Her struggles were futile and terror was threatening to overwhelm her. That this could happen. . . One minute before and she'd been safe. . .

The man gave a drunken laugh. 'You'll never get me to gaol. I got thirty witnesses says I was over the other side of town. Now, shut up, bitch.' He reached the edge of the gravel and shoved her down.

'Leave her alone.'

A voice rang out from the back of the pack of bikes. It was young, defiant, and sounded as terrified as Gina. Gina's assailant stiffened. As Gina struggled to rise he hit her hard, forcing her back to the ground. Then he stood over her, looking back towards the bikers.

'Who the hell said that?'

A youth was pushing his way through the bikers. Gina twisted somehow and saw him through a haze of terror. A youth. . . He was twenty years old, maybe. . . He'd shoved off his helmet to reveal a shock of blond hair, and in the light of the massed headlights the boy's face was ashen. 'Leave her alone,' he said. 'If you rape her then I'll go to the police. She's right when she says you'll go to gaol.'

'You little——' The man gave Gina a swift kick, as if putting her on hold, reached out and grabbed the youth by the lapel of his leather jacket. 'I don't know you,' he said slowly, hauling him up to face him. 'Who the hell are you?'

'He's not one of us,' one of the other riders called out. 'Just rode in after us. He's right, though. Geez, Mick, leave the broad alone. We got enough trouble. . .'

'Shut up.'

Gina was crawling sideways, out of range. She got about two feet before Mick saw. With an oath he kicked out again. His boot sliced into her thigh, shoving her back down into the dust. 'You move and I'll kill you,' he told her. 'Stay where you are while I deal with this.' He hauled the boy closer to him.

The boy didn't have a chance. He was tall but slightly built—only half the bulk of Mick. Mick lifted his body clear off the ground and thrust him backwards, back, until there was only the safety rail. . .

The drop went for hundreds of feet. Gina gave a low moan. She hauled herself frantically up but another of the bikers stepped forward to restrain her.

'Keep still, sweetheart. If you know what's good for you. . .'

'I should let my dog at you,' Mick was saying to the boy. 'But I don't think I will. I don't. . .'

With a savage shove he thrust the boy backwards.

There was a sharp, dreadful scream, the sound of a body smashing into the cliff-face below, and then silence.

'What the hell. . .?' The man holding Gina let her go and strode forward. 'Mick, you've killed him.' His voice sounded dead scared. 'You fool. Laying a broad's one thing, but murder. . .'

'If you don't like it, you can clear off.' Mick shouted, but there was an edge of fear to his voice. The sound of the body crashing into rock still seemed to echo. It was as if he'd just realised what he'd done.

'Yeah, I will,' the other biker said. 'And if you have any sense you will too.' The man strode back to his bike. Without a backward look he mounted and gunned the motor into life.

'You can't. . .' Fear was deepening in Mick's voice.

'Watch us.' Another of the bikers. Bikes were revving and the bikers were moving—fast—getting as far from this as possible.

Moments later there was only Gina and Mick left on the mountain.

The big biker stood staring at her, and Gina knew instinctively what he was thinking. She could see it in his eyes. He'd committed murder and Gina was witness.

He was walking slowly towards her, blocking her way to the car. She backed away, ignoring the knifing pain in her hip. 'Stay where you are, bitch,' he growled. 'Move and I'll set the dog on you.' He smashed out with his hand and she fell.

And then a headlight turned back into the clearing. Another bike. . . A mate of Mick's, returned to help him?

Gina was beyond sound. She knelt in the blaze of headlight, her hands held up in a futile gesture of defence. Defence? She had none.

The motor of the new bike died. A man dismounted—a man every bit the size of Mick. Bigger. . . Like Mick, he wore black leathers, but his at least were clean and unmarked. A black helmet covered his head, and the only part of him visible was a huge black beard.

'What the hell's going on?'

A tiny flicker of hope. He didn't know. . .

'Clear out of what's not your business,' Mick growled.

The bearded man looked down at Gina. 'Are you OK?' It was plain as day that she wasn't.

'N——' How on earth to get her voice to work? 'No. He's going to kill me. He's already killed——'

'Shut up, bitch.' Mick turned, lifted a hand and slashed down hard across her face, but even as his hand made contact the newcomer moved. Gina was somehow flung clear.

The newcomer hit Mick with a blow that thudded with sickening force. Mick reeled back, but another blow followed. Mick fell, and the dog launched itself straight at the newcomer.

Blackbeard hadn't expected it, but his helmet protected his face. He put up his hands in an attempt to ward off the vicious jaws fighting to reach his neck. Behind the dog, Mick slowly staggered to his feet. A malicious grin twisted his face. Pit bulls were killers.

There was only one way this could go if the dog stayed in the fight. One man against a murderer and a killer dog. . . One man and Gina. . .

So she couldn't stay crouched, sobbing with the pain in her leg. 'Come on, woman. . . Move. . .' She whispered the words to herself. Somehow she struggled to her feet and looked frantically around.

There was an old picnic table a few feet away. The top was made of four slats of wood, and one of them had come away. If it pulled free. . .

She launched herself at it as if it were life itself. Blessedly, the wood lifted.

'Here!' she screamed. She couldn't see where man stopped and dog started. If Blackbeard turned. . .gave her room between him and the dog. . .

He saw her uplifted hands—the wooden slat upraised like a sword. The dog had hold of his arm, gripping like death. With an oath the man ripped his leather jacket from his arms and swung it in a wide arc around towards Gina. The dog flew. . .

Now! She wasn't sure who screamed it. . . Or maybe no one screamed it at all. The wooden slat swung high, higher and down. . .

There was only this one chance. Pit bulls were bred for fighting. Fighting to the death. She put all her strength into the blow—as if she too were bred for fighting—and the dog was dead before it hit the ground.

Gina had never killed anything in her life before, and the sensation made her sick to the stomach. She loved dogs. . . The pit bull lay lifeless on the ground, its teeth still meshed in Blackbeard's jacket.

Which left Mick as the only threat. . .

Mick's support had been cut from under him. His dog was dead, his mates were gone, and so was his swaggering courage. He stood breathing heavily, staring from Blackbeard to Gina and back again.

Blackbeard hadn't finished. He walked across to Mick's bike. The key was still in the ignition. Blackbeard lifted it, stared at it for a long moment as if coming to a decision, and then hurled it as far into the night as he could, over the safety rail and down into the valley below.

The same way as the boy. . .

The boy. . . Gina gave a choking sob and stumbled to the rail. There was nothing there. An endless drop, and darkness.

Behind her she was vaguely aware of Blackbeard hauling his helmet off, revealing a harsh-boned face, deep black hair and eyes that still held murder. Anger emanated in waves, and Mick saw it. There was no understanding here. No quarter for Mick. Blackbeard stared straight at Mick as he lifted a mobile phone from his pocket.

A phone, for heaven's sake. . .

One click. A pre-set number. 'Maggie, I need police and ambulance up at Skene's Look-out.' It was a strong, commanding voice, seemingly sure that the unknown Maggie would follow orders. 'Now, Maggie. Priority One.' The telephone was clipped away.

'I'll kill you. . .' Mick was having trouble with his speech. A thin trickle of blood was oozing down his chin.

'You'd better hurry, then.' Blackbeard sounded profoundly uninterested in anything Mick might say. 'The police are on their way.'

Mick stared in baffled, drunken fury. The police. . .

The word finally sank in. Police. And he'd killed a man.

The last trace of bluff sagged out of him. There was only his useless bike and his dead dog left. And Blackbeard. . .

He turned and stumbled from the clearing, and thirty seconds later he was gone.

'The police will pick him up.' The same uninterested voice. Blackbeard crossed to where Gina was standing and put a hand on her shoulder. 'You're safe now.' He stared down, and then his hand dropped to her thigh. The way she'd moved told him she was injured and there was blood seeping through the denim of her jeans. He lifted his hand and it was stained red. His lips tightened and the anger intensified. She could feel it surging.

'But. . .' Gina was shaking like a leaf. Her voice wobbled. She took a deep breath. She had to make herself say it. 'But. . .he's over the cliff. . .'

'He?'

'There's a boy. . . Mick threw him over the rail. . .'

For one long moment he stared at her. The headlights of the two bikes were still on. They showed Blackbeard a girl whose eyes were too big for her face. A bruise was already starting to swell across her eye, and the skin had split on her eyebrow. Gina pushed a hand up to lift her hair away from her eyes. She must look like a real biker's moll.

'A boy?' he said blankly.

'They were going. . . They were going to rape me. And the boy. . .he wasn't one of them. He tried to stop them. But there were so many. . . And Mick. . . Mick threw him down. . .'

'Lloyd. . .' The word was hardly a whisper. Blackbeard's hands came up and tightened so hard on her shoulders that she cried out. 'Dear God,' he groaned. 'It must be Lloyd. What does he look like?'

'Tall. Fair. . .fair hair. Thin. . .' Gina pulled back from his hands. 'Please. . .let me go. If I can get down to him. . .'

He released her as if she were electrically charged. 'It'll be Lloyd.' His voice was dully certain. He moved back towards the cliff-edge. 'There's a way down. Stay here. Direct the ambulance.' He shoved aside a bush beside the safety rail and dropped from view.

Direct the ambulance. . .

Gina stood motionless for perhaps ten seconds as she collected her thoughts. There were two bikes with headlights shining straight over the cliff. Her car was here, with door still agape. If the ambulance officers couldn't guess where they were. . .

She could go too. She was a doctor, for heaven's sake, and if by some miracle the boy wasn't dead. . . By some miracle. . .

She was having trouble making her leg work. It felt numb.

'That's nothing to what will be wrong with him,' she muttered fiercely as she crossed to the car. Her bag was in the boot. Maybe. . . Maybe it could be useful. If he was still alive. . .

Please God, let it be useful. The boy had been thrown over the cliff because he had tried to save her. The thought made her feel dizzy. She grabbed her bag, pushed aside Blackbeard's bush and searched for the path.

It was hardly a path. The drop was almost vertical, but here, at least, there were outcrops of rock where Gina could get a foothold. If the moon hadn't been full it would have been impossible. As it was. . . As it was she fell a dozen times before she finally made out a crouched figure stooping over a body.

He hadn't fallen the whole way. The cliff itself wasn't absolutely vertical. She could see that from here, though it hadn't been clear from the top. There were ledges, and places where the slope was steep but not straight down. The boy had fallen and rolled forty feet or so. Enough. . .

Blackbeard was kneeling over the boy, and he was swearing. A low, steady stream of invective cut through the night. The boy was absolutely still.

Gina dropped her bag. Without speaking she moved to the other side of the boy and touched his wrist.

A pulse. . .

She looked up to Blackbeard, and his face in the moonlight told her that he was personally involved. The injured boy must be Lloyd, then. A relation? Younger brother, maybe? The man's face was bleak as mid-winter.

'He's alive,' she said gently.

'I know he's alive.' His voice caught in rigid anger. 'I told you to stay——'

'I'm a doctor.' Gina was no longer looking at him. Her attention was all on the boy. He was buckled over. If he'd landed like that. . .

She could feel Blackbeard's shock. 'A doctor?'

'Yes.' She said it as much to reassure him as anything. Not that there was much reassuring about the boy's condition. 'I'm Dr Gina Buchanan. I'm on my way to visit my fiancé at Gundowring.'

'Yeah?' Disbelief. 'And you just stopped off for a

tryst with your biker-friends on the way?'

The words were savage, but Gina ignored them. She'd coped with relatives in shock before and this man was showing every sign. She lifted her blouse and ripped.

'What the hell. . .?'

'He's bleeding.' She'd put her hand on the rock near the base of the boy's spine and found it warm and sticky. Her fingers had located a tear in the denim of his jeans, and she could feel blood spurting from a torn artery. 'He's torn his leg. There's massive bleeding on his thigh.'

'Don't move him.'

Blackbeard's voice was raised in warning, and Gina nodded. The man knew basic first aid, then.

'I won't,' she promised. 'The ambulance will bring a stretcher we can use to immobilise him. Meanwhile, I'll make a pressure-pad. The last thing he needs is to lose any more blood.' She looked ruefully down at the material she'd ripped. The damned blouse was so flimsy. 'I need some of yours too.'

'What?'

'Some of your shirt. To make a pad.'

'A pad. . . Oh, yeah. . .' As if collecting himself, he hauled off his shirt and ripped.

The man was so big. . . Even in shock, with pain shooting from her thigh straight down her leg and her fear for the boy making her feel sick, Gina was aware of his body. His bare torso was muscled and tanned. A body most bikers would kill for. . .

What was she thinking of? With a jolt she hauled herself back to what she was doing. She took the proffered cloth and moved her hand carefully under the ripped denim, easing her fingers slowly so she wouldn't shift him a fraction of an inch. Then she pressed hard down, one hand above the other. There was pressure over the wound but he was kept absolutely still.

'I'll do it.' Blackbeard sounded as sick as she was.

'No.' Gina shook her head. He might be able to apply more pressure but she knew just where to press. She knew what she was doing. 'I can get enough pressure,' she told him, and then stiffened.

The boy's body had shifted imperceptibly. It was almost as if a tremor had passed through him. She looked up and the boy's eyes flicked open.

'Don't try to move,' she said urgently. She looked up at Blackbeard. 'Hold his shoulders and reassure. . .'

There was no need. Blackbeard was already applying gentle pressure to the boy's upper body, preventing instinctive movement.

'Lloyd. . .' His voice was unsteady. 'Lloyd. . .'

'Struan. . .' It was a whisper from a long way away.

'I'm here. Just lie still, you young fool, till we try and find out the damage.'

'There was a girl. . .'

'And a knight in shining armour.' Blackbeard grimaced. 'And you never could resist a dragon.'

'Is she OK? They didn't. . .?'

'I'm right here.' Gina's voice shook. She shifted slightly, so he could see her in the moonlight. 'I'm fine. Thanks to you.'

'They didn't rape. . .?'

'You scared them. They took off.'

It was as much as he needed to know—that his effort hadn't been in vain. He closed his eyes. There was intense pain—Gina could see it in the tight set of his mouth.

Her bag was behind her. 'There's morphine in my bag,' she told Blackbeard. 'Can you open it?' Her hands were fully occupied. She couldn't move now until the stretcher arrived. How the heck was she going to inject him? She'd just have to talk Blackbeard through a muscular injection. It wouldn't be as effective as intravenous. . .

'Your bag. . .?' Blackbeard stared up in amazement and his eyes swung behind her. 'Your bag.' The repeated words were a prayer of thankfulness. He reached over and pulled it towards him, flicking it open in one swift movement.

Gina stared. The lock on her bag was tricky—designed to stop inquisitive fingers. This man had dealt with such locks before. He hauled the bag open and in ten seconds was holding up a morphine ampoule and a syringe, for all the world as if he knew exactly what to do with them.

Was he an addict? Heaven alone knew, she thought bleakly. On the up-side, at least the man could give an injection.

'Show me the ampoule,' she ordered. 'He needs ten milligrams.'

'Five, intravenously.'

'But you can't——' Gina stopped. The man had found a swab in her bag and was pulling off the boy's leather glove. He washed down the back of his hand in seconds. 'What. . .what the heck are you doing?'

'What does it look like?' he snapped. 'Five milligrams intravenously and another five in ten minutes if it's not enough.' The man was snapping the glass vial and filling the syringe.

'Show me the ampoule.' Gina was cringing inside. She was so helpless. Her hands tied her exactly where she was, and if he made a mistake. . . 'There's a flashlight in the side of my bag. I want to see the ampoule.'

'It's OK, Dr Buchanan. I know what I'm doing.' He was taking no notice of her at all. The syringe was filled, his fingers smoothed back the boy's hand as he checked the chosen vein, and the needle was in place before she could protest further. Gina was left with open mouth and nothing to say.

Dear God. . . She hadn't even seen the ampoule. . .

If he'd made a mistake. . . 'Do you. . .? Are you sure it was the morphine?'

'It's a bit late to ask that now.' Blackbeard flicked the cap safely back on the exposed needle and placed it back in the bag. Then he took Lloyd's hand. 'That's morphine going home, Lloyd. You know how fast that works. Any minute now and the pain will ease. . .'

'It'd want to. . .' The boy's voice cracked and his eyes flicked wide again. 'Struan, I can't feel my legs.'

'It's no bloody wonder. You've bruised your back by falling close on forty feet. With that bruising. . .'

'I can't feel my legs. . .' It was a sob of terror and Gina winced. Once more she looked at the rock the boy had smashed into—and the way his back was bent.

'It's far too soon for fear,' Struan was saying. 'You know as well as anyone that bruising of the spine can cause temporary loss of feeling. We'll keep you absolutely still, though.'

'Struan. . .'

'Can you feel the morphine working?' It was an attempt to make the boy think of something other than his legs, and as a ruse it worked.

'Yes. . . Yes, I can. . .' Lloyd's voice drifted away from them. 'Yes. . .'

He'd lost so much blood. . . 'Can you. . .can you put pressure here, please?' Gina managed. She desperately wanted to free a hand so she could check his pulse. Blackbeard was before her, though. He lifted the boy's wrist.

'It's OK. . .' She could tell by his voice that it wasn't.

'There's adrenalin in my bag.' Good grief. . . She was treating the man like a doctor.

'A saline drip?'

She stared. 'Are you. . .?'

'A doctor? Of course I am.' He was fumbling in her bag. 'Do you carry saline?'

'The base of the bag lifts up.' Gina's breath came

out in a rush. 'There's a saline bag there.' She sat back, the tension easing. A doctor. . . It meant the responsibility had shifted. She could sit here and stop the boy bleeding to death and let someone else worry. She could give in to the throbbing pain in her thigh. . .

'You let that pressure off and we're in trouble.' Blackbeard's voice was harsh, hauling her back to what she had to do. Gina nodded. He'd seen her shoulders sag.

A doctor. . . She watched as Blackbeard's skilful fingers prepared the boy's arm and set up the saline drip. There was no stand. He balanced the bag on his shoulder as he worked.

A doctor? A doctor with a beard like that? A doctor who tore around the country on a Harley Davidson?

Lloyd was no longer with them. The morphine had taken effect. That and the shock had sent him drifting into blessed unconsciousness.

'There's. . .there's a blanket in my car,' she managed. Blackbeard would have to go. Her hands were still needed.

'No.'

'No?'

'If I leave I risk you passing out.'

Gina took a deep breath. 'I won't faint,' she said with dignity. 'I never faint.'

'How many times in your life have you had this type of thing happen?'

Once. . . Once before in Gina's life there had been a night where things had been right out of control.

She hadn't fainted then either. Just sat by herself, for hour upon endless hour, and made a vow. . .

'I won't faint,' she repeated. 'I promise. You can go.'

He didn't have to. There was the sound of a car's engine—wheels skidding to a halt in the car park above them. A siren approaching from a distance, and then more cars. . .

'Here comes the cavalry.' Blackbeard lifted Lloyd's limp hand. 'Here's help, Lloyd, lad. Hold on, now.' He was talking to himself.

CHAPTER TWO

WITH the arrival of medical assistance Gina was superfluous. The ambulance officers set up floodlights and clambered down the cliff in minutes. Police, too. Lloyd was moved skilfully on to a stretcher, his position not changed by so much as an inch. Four policemen, two ambulance officers and Blackbeard worked to lift the stretcher to the top.

They winched from above, with three men holding the stretcher steady as it rose. That way there was no jolting at all.

There was nothing for Gina to do. She sat at the rear of the ledge and let the events of the last thirty minutes catch up with her. Now she was no longer needed. . .

Her body was trembling and she felt sick. Waves of nausea were washing over her, and she shoved her head down between her knees.

'I never faint,' she told herself desperately, but she knew she was close to it now. Finally, as the men and stretcher moved upward, she rose to her feet. She had to follow. The pain in her thigh shot through her body like fire. She took a step, and then another. . .

The floodlights were lighting the entire cliff. Blackbeard was holding the saline bag as the stretcher lifted over the cliff-top and he glanced back down to see Gina sink to her knees. With an oath he handed over the bag to one of the men operating the winch and descended swiftly.

'And just how badly are you hurt, Dr Buchanan?' He crossed swiftly to kneel beside her.

His tone had changed. The desperate worry of a few

moments ago had been supplanted by professionalism. Gina had heard this tone before. She'd used
it herself when coping with sick and frightened
children.

'I'll be fine.' She raised a sickly white face to his.
'Please. . .the boy. . .'

'Lloyd is in good hands.' As Blackbeard spoke the
ambulance doors slammed shut on the cliff-top and
the motor started. 'He'll be in hospital in moments
and they're radioing in to Casualty to have them
expect him.'

'Th—there's a doctor there?'

'Martin Wisehart's at the hospital. He's had orthopaedic training and he's good.'

'You should go with him.'

'I've more than one patient.' Blackbeard had
supported her to a sitting position. Then, as faces
appeared over the cliff to find out the hold-up, he
yelled upward. 'Take the ambulance in, but I need a
lift here, boys.'

'I can walk. . .'

'Don't be stupid.' He touched her leg and noted the
pain flash across her face. 'How the hell did you get
down here?' He hadn't seen her descend. He'd been
too preoccupied with Lloyd.

'I can't remember,' Gina said truthfully. She dredged
up a smile. 'I think I might have rolled.'

'You must have, with this leg.' He was peering down,
a flashlight donated by one of the policemen in his
hand. 'I knew it was cut, but. . .I'm going to rip your
jeans a bit further. Hold on.'

'Don't mind me,' Gina winced. 'You're the second
man tonight. . .'

He flashed her a grin. 'Good girl. If you can still
laugh. . .' He watched her face as he pulled the already
ripped jeans further apart over her thigh. A ragged
tear was still bleeding sluggishly and the whole area

around it was a mass of haematoma—bleeding into muscle. 'My God. . .'

'You're not supposed to say that. I want you to say. . ."Is that all? What a fuss about nothing, Dr Buchanan."'

He smiled absently. 'Is that all. . .' he started, as he inspected the injured flesh. He looked up at her face again, and his face lost its humour. His mouth set in a grim, angry line. 'The bastard. . .'

'I don't think it's broken,' Gina whispered. 'It's stiffening but I can still move it. . .'

'Yeah. . .' He grabbed her bag, still lying beside her. 'You wouldn't have made it down here with a break this high. Have you any more painkiller?'

'I don't need——'

'Just shut up, Dr Buchanan. If you want a job in this valley. . .'

If she wanted a job. . . Gina froze. A job. . . That was a hope for the future. 'A job. . .?'

'You are intending to practise in Gundowring?' he demanded. 'Or are you here to marry and raise babies?'

In spite of the pain, Gina managed a wan smile. 'Both, I hope.'

'Good for you.' He flashed her a concerned look as his fingers snapped open a vial of morphine.

'Look, I really don't need——'

'You really need. Who's the lucky man?'

'Wayne. . . Wayne Macky. He's the administrator at the hospital.'

His fingers stopped. For a fraction of a moment his face went blank, and then he collected himself.

'Wayne. . . Well, well. I wouldn't have thought the boy had it in him.'

'He's no boy.'

Humour flashed back into Blackbeard's eyes. 'No.' Gina could see Blackbeard conjuring up a vision of thirty-six-year-old Wayne—complete with balding head and the beginnings of a paunch. 'No, I guess he's not.'

He'd know him well, Gina thought. Wayne was chief administrator for the hospital where this man must work. . . Maybe he'd know him as well as she did?

'And where did you meet our Wayne?' He was swabbing the back of her hand. In one swift movement the syringe went home. A tiny pain, but Gina sagged. Blackbeard swore, and took her shoulders in his strong grip. 'Hold on now, sweetheart. Help's coming.' From above there was the sound of the ambulance moving off and then men clambering down the cliff again. 'Have you been in Gundowring before?'

He was trying to keep her mind off the pain until the morphine worked. The same technique he had used for Lloyd. . .

'I've never been to Gundowring. And I've known Wayne since. . .since I was a child. . .' Her voice hardly seemed to belong to her.

'Lucky you.'

'Yes.' Gina was suddenly defensive. 'I am lucky.'

Blackbeard smiled. 'I don't doubt it, Dr Buchanan.' His grip on her tightened. 'And so, I'm beginning to think, is Wayne.'

Gina subsided. She couldn't think of anything to say.

Seconds later a policeman was crouched beside them.

'Will we ring for another ambulance, Doc?' the officer asked, taking in the situation at a glance.

'No. She'll be OK in the back seat of a car if we can get her up.'

'I can walk.'

'And pigs can fly,' Blackbeard smiled, and his smile was so tender that it did something funny to Gina's middle. He lifted each of her arms, watching her face.

'No damage? I don't want to lift you and then discover you've a dislocated shoulder.'

'My arms are fine.' Dignified, but her words sounded odd. Slurred.

'Pretty nice arms, I'd say. Wouldn't you, Doc?' The big policeman, at a gesture from Blackbeard, was crouching by Gina's other side. As one they rose, with Gina supported by both shoulders. Their hands linked under the base of her spine and Gina realised there were professionals at work here. A fireman's hold. She was slight enough for one of them to carry over flat ground, but not up this treacherous slope.

Two big men who'd done this before. She felt powerless—and cared for—as their arms linked underneath her and around her shoulders. The feeling was novel and not altogether unpleasant.

'Pretty good package,' Blackbeard grinned, his arms tightening around his patient. He gestured to Gina's bag with his eyes. 'Can one of your boys retrieve this?' he asked the policeman.

'Sure. We'll be sticking around.' They were slowly, carefully moving up the cliff-face as the policeman spoke. Lit by floodlight from above, it wasn't impossible, but they had to watch their feet. 'We'll see if we can't locate our friend. . .'

'Mick. . .' Gina made her tongue work. 'His name was Mick.'

'We know,' the policeman told her. 'Michael Gray Carter. We just got the radio-check on the bike's registration. The man's got a police record as long as your arm. We kicked him and his friends out of the camping-grounds earlier tonight. Escorted them to the town boundary a couple of hours ago—but it seems it wasn't far enough. We'll pick him up now, though. There's only bush on the mountain, and clear paddocks beneath. Without wheels, he can't have got far. It's a matter of sitting and waiting for him to come out.'

The big policeman smiled. 'And we can wait a very long time.'

Gina didn't respond. The morphine was working. She felt safe. The pain in her hip was easing, although the jolting over the rough ground didn't help. Even so, it had faded to a dull, aching grind. Bearable. . .

Finally they reached the top. Gina was carried over to the police car. It was the biggest, most comfortable vehicle on the cliff-top.

'I'll borrow this and take her straight in,' Blackbeard was saying. It was all Gina could do to hear. She was drifting in a drug-induced haze, her body cradled by the leather of the car's upholstery. Anyone could do anything with her now. She no longer cared. 'Can you organise Dr Buchanan's car and my bike?'

'Sure, Doc.' The policeman frowned. 'Did you say Dr Buchanan?'

'Yeah.' Blackbeard smiled down at Gina. 'Seems the valley has a new doctor.'

There was a moment's silence. The policeman's mouth set.

'That's a handy coincidence,' he grimaced. 'Throw one down a cliff and pick up a new one!'

Gina woke to a hospital bed.

The drive down to Gundowring Hospital was a haze. She remembered snatches. . . Blackbeard's face, set and grim as he concentrated on the curves down the steep mountain road, the bright lights of Casualty entrance, nurses stripping her and people exclaiming over her leg.

Wayne had been somewhere there, his face white with shock and concern as he leaned over her bed, his voice fussing over a private room. A policeman asking questions, herself trying to think, asking about Lloyd and no one saying, and then Blackbeard, telling them to get the hell out of the ward, that she'd had enough and he was giving her something to sleep.

And now. . .

It was morning. The sun was flickering in through the window, throwing brilliant patterns over the white counterpane. She moved her head to look out of the window and her neck hurt. The sea shimmered in the distance. It was worth hurting her neck to see.

The door swung open and a nurse popped her head around.

'Oh, you're awake,' she smiled. 'Lovely. How do you feel?'

Gina considered. The stab of pain in her neck had subsided. If she just lay really, really still. . .

'Would you like to be propped up on some pillows so you can have some breakfast?'

A difficult decision. 'I don't know,' she said cautiously.

'It'll do you good.' The door had swung open again and Gina stared.

Blackbeard.

It was a different Blackbeard from the night before, though. The man last night had been a biker who said he was a doctor. This man. . . This man was a professional. He was dressed in tailored trousers, open-necked shirt and a generous white coat. A stethoscope hung from his top pocket. His black curls were neatly brushed and only his huge black beard looked the least bit disreputable.

His eyes looked the same. Gina looked up to the man's deep grey-black eyes. They were what she remembered from the night before—eyes filled with compassion and caring, with the trace of humour lurking behind the laugh-lines.

'Good morning.' His eyes smiled down at her and the strange feeling that she'd felt the night before lurched back. As if she wasn't quite sure what her heart was doing.

'G-good morning.'

He crossed to her chart and picked it up. 'Decided to live then, have we?'

'I never threatened otherwise.'

'No.' Once again that damned smile. 'You didn't. Though if you'd had your way you'd have been left to bleed to death on the mountain. Bloody independent females.'

'I didn't lose that much blood.'

'A fair bit,' he told her. 'We've put fifteen stitches in your thigh.'

'Fifteen. . .' Gina gasped. She lifted her bedcover and tried to look down but her neck jabbed.

He saw her wince. His hand came down to touch her face lightly, with fingers that were infinitely gentle.

'We'll get you a mirror. Sister, could you. . .?'

The nurse nodded and went out. Blackbeard settled himself on the end of the bed and looked at her.

'Well, then.' He smiled. 'I don't think we made formal introductions last night. I'm Struan Maitland. And you're Dr Gina Buchanan, I presume?'

'Yes.' Of course. Struan. . . Not Blackbeard, then. His name seemed to have disappeared along with his leathers. She flushed and looked under the covers again.

'You won't be able to see without a mirror. But there's no lasting damage. A nasty cut, and bleeding into muscle. Massive bruising. What footballers refer to as a cork thigh. I'm keeping you in bed for a couple of days to let it subside, or I risk a clot. If you're agreeable I'll bring our local magistrate in for a look later on.'

Our local magistrate. . .? Gina lay back and her eyes narrowed. 'Oh, yes? And the jury? Twelve good men and true checking out what's under my hospital gown?'

He grinned. 'Hardly that. Our magistrate is Janet Leith. You'll like her, and I promise she won't take liberties. Though she might want a photograph.'

'Oh, feel free. . .'

'Feeling a wee bit exposed, are we, Dr Buchanan?' She glared. 'Wouldn't you?'

His smile faded. 'Yes.' Once again his fingers touched her face. 'Yes, I would. Gina, there'll be a policeman along later this morning to go through exactly what happened. . .'

'Will he want a look too?'

'I promise I won't let him.' He frowned down at the bruising on her face. 'Though he can see a lot from here.' His smile didn't return. 'He really did hurt you.'

The unspoken question lay between them. It had to be asked. Gina took a deep breath.

'And. . .and Lloyd?'

The last vestige of laughter faded from Blackbeard's eyes. 'We airlifted Lloyd to Melbourne this morning. He's fractured his spine at D12.'

'Fracture. . .' Gina found her fingers were clenching into her palms under the bedclothes. 'Unstable. . .?'

'It's too soon to tell. It looks stable, but there's no feeling below the break at all. He should be arriving in Melbourne about now. Martin Wisehart, our orthopaedic surgeon, has gone with him. He'll contact me as soon as he knows.'

Silence. The sister was taking her time finding a mirror.

'Tell me. . .tell me about Lloyd,' Gina whispered. She looked up at the doctor. 'You. . .you do know him? I wasn't imagining it?'

'Lloyd Neale is a resident here.'

'Resident. . .' Gina frowned. 'Medical resident?'

The man shrugged. 'Yes. Lloyd is six months into his second medical residence year. He's the best resident this hospital has ever had—a fine young man. He's going to make a brilliant physician some day.' He grimaced. 'If the fates permit.'

'A doctor. . .' Gina thought back. 'He seemed. . . He seems so young.'

'I guess that's because he was scared silly. You seemed about sixteen last night too, and I gather you're considerably older?'

It was a question. 'I'm twenty-eight,' Gina told him, and watched his eyebrows lift in surprise.

'Twenty-eight. . . So, not a sprig just out of medical school?'

'No.'

'So what has Dr Buchanan been doing for the last few years while she waited for Mr Right?'

Gina's eyes moved swiftly to his. A hint of irony was behind the words. Wayne. . . Mr Right. . .

She'd have to get used to it. She'd made her decision. 'I've been training as a paediatrician.'

'You're kidding?'

'No.' Gina's eyes stayed steady.

'You're qualified?'

'Yes.'

He stood up then, and walked to the window. His hands dug deep into the pockets of his white coat as he stared out across the distant ocean. 'You could have told us you were coming.'

'Why?' Gina's head was deep in her pillows. She was warm and secure and sleepy. . . Drug-induced sleepiness. 'I decided to marry Wayne, so I'd take my chances. If there wasn't a hospital job then I'd set up my own practice. Or, if not. . .' She smiled suddenly. 'I thought, if not I could have a few babies of my own.'

'You and Wayne. . .?'

'Of course, me and Wayne.' Funny, though, in her equation Wayne hadn't really come into it. A base from which to work. Security.

'We're a doctor short now.'

'Because of Lloyd.' Gina flinched. 'I'm not taking Lloyd's job.'

'Even if it's the least you could do for him?'

Gina's eyes widened. 'What do you mean?'

'I mean that Lloyd is going to be out of action for at least a couple of months. Assuming the best case scenario, and that the break is stable, the bruising has been enough to cause paralysis. This morning there was no feeling at all. You know as well as anyone that it'll take time to recover, if it ever does.'

'So. . .'

'So we have to have a resident, or equivalent. We can't hold Lloyd's job—your precious administrator was making noises about it only this morning. If we ask for another resident we'll be assigned one permanently and Lloyd will be sent somewhere else if. . . when he recovers. And, frankly, we want Lloyd here. Long-term. So I'm suggesting you hold Lloyd's job, let us have a chance to check you out, and then, if things work out, we broaden the practice to include a paediatrician.'

'A resident. . .'

'I'm not suggesting we treat you like a resident. You'll be given as much responsibility as you like. It'll only be your salary that won't reflect your qualifications.'

Wayne wouldn't like that. . .

He could see what she was thinking. Blackbeard. . . His name was Struan. She would have to cut out calling him Blackbeard or she'd do it to his face. Struan grinned. 'Your Wayne would be the last person to suggest we pay you paediatric wages,' he said. 'Very intent on cost-cutting, is your Wayne.'

Gina's eyes narrowed. A neat way to get back at Wayne?

'You don't like him?' she said flatly.

'Your fiancé? No, I don't.' He grimaced, and then smiled again, that same, damned, heart-stopping smile. 'But then I haven't just promised to marry him. Each to his own, Dr Buchanan, or her own, as the case may be.' He looked around as the door opened and the nurse appeared. 'Ah. Your mirror, my lady. Let's inspect the damage, shall we?'

Her leg was horrible. Immune as Gina had become to trauma, on her own body it was different. The mass of angry purple, with the jagged tear running through the centre, made her feel sick to the stomach. Blackbeard. . .Struan. . .had made a neat job of stitching, but she'd have a fine scar for the rest of her life.

'You really will have to rest it,' he told her. 'With this amount of bruising it's dangerous not to. You've the odd torn muscle in there as well. You'll need crutches for a week or so.'

'Great.'

'It's the best we can do.'

She flashed a look up to him. He had sounded apologetic.

'I'm sorry.' She shook her head. 'I don't sound grateful.' She swallowed. 'I really am—very, very grateful. You and Lloyd. . . Well, you saved my life.'

'You didn't do too bad a job yourself. If you hadn't killed the dog. . .'

The dog. Gina winced and put a hand up to her eyes. The memory made her feel even sicker.

'You had no choice,' Struan said gently, sensing her distress. 'It would have killed me.'

'Only because it was trained to. . .'

'I know. But once trained to kill. . . There was no option but to do what you did.' He stood up and picked up the mirror. 'You've had a dog yourself then, Dr Buchanan?'

'Once. . .' Gina thought back and the memory lightened. 'A long time ago.' Part of the haze of the 'before' time.

'Maybe you should think about another. For the long

winter evenings when Wayne's absorbed in his chess.'

'Chess?'

'Our Wayne's a whiz at chess. I would have thought you knew that. He plays three nights a week. Though I don't suppose he'll do that now you've come. . .' Struan looked down the corridor. 'And speaking of whizzes. . .here's our Wayne.' He threw Gina an expressive look that held—of all things—sympathy, and left her to her visitor.

Wayne. . .

It was a warm day, but Wayne was wearing his work uniform. Neat three-piece suit, in correct navy with expensive pale blue silk tie. He crossed and kissed Gina on the forehead, carefully avoiding the dressing over her injured eye.

'Gina, love. . .'

She relaxed. Wayne was as familiar as an old slipper. Their respective mothers had been friends, and Wayne, eight years older than Gina, had kept in touch with her afterwards. Once a month, without fail, Wayne had visited. It was the only continuity she had had in her succession of foster homes. Wayne had fulfilled his obligations with diligence, and Gina was never forgotten. It was only later that Gina realised the monthly visits had turned into an expectation.

'You frightened the life out of me.'

He didn't look as if his life had been threatened. He looked smug, Gina decided as he pulled up the chair beside her bed. As though things were going right.

'I'm sorry you got such a shock.'

'I guess you got a bigger one.' He smiled fondly down at her. 'Though I must say, Gina, that pulling off the road after dark was a crazy thing to do. Especially with the town full of bikers.'

'How could I have guessed——?'

'We have a biker convention here every year,'

Wayne told her. 'A huge swap-meet. It's great for business here because of the brawls and accidents. A real boost to the coffers.'

'Whoopee,' Gina said drily, but Wayne didn't hear her.

'There are some who say bikers aren't all bad,' Wayne said darkly. 'Drs Maitland and Neale, for instance. They both ride Harley Davidsons and wear leathers. And look what comes of it.'

'They saved my life.'

'And if we'd banned the swap-meet they wouldn't have had to. If I had my way there'd be no motorbikes permitted in the town.'

'There's plenty of decent people ride motorbikes,' Gina protested. 'There are morons behind the wheels of cars too.'

He lifted his eyebrows and forbore to comment, and Gina knew that he was humouring a sick woman.

'It's an ill wind though. . .' He smiled. 'Has Dr Maitland offered you the job?'

'Yes.' Gina's face froze.

'Well, if this hadn't happened. . .I can't see us justifying another doctor at the moment, but with Lloyd gone they'll need you. And if he's permanently paralysed. . .'

'Wayne. . .' Despite the stab of pain down her leg Gina pushed herself to a sitting position. 'Wayne, Lloyd saved my life. He was hurt trying to get those morons off me. If he's paralysed. . . How can you possibly be pleased that we'll gain?'

'I'm not pleased.' Wayne's blue eyes widened in innocence. 'All I'm saying is that it'll make it easier for us. Two salaries. . . There's a nice brick veneer up on the headland I want you to see as soon as you're up to it.'

Gina sank back. Her anger faded. Maybe it would be OK.

'The police are coming in soon,' Wayne told her. He stood. 'I can't be long.'

Great. She wanted him to go.

'I suppose. . .' He looked down at her, his face solemn. 'I suppose you didn't encourage them in any way, did you, Gina? They'll be asking. I mean. . . Just be careful in what you tell them.'

'Encourage. . .' Gina's face went blank.

'Well. . .' His eyes met hers and he smiled, a proprietorial and smug grin. 'You're a very good-looking woman. Everybody in the hospital has been telling me so all morning. It wouldn't take much. . .'

'I didn't encourage them in any way,' Gina said flatly. She bit her lip. 'Wayne. . .'

'Yes, my love?'

'Go away. I want to go to sleep.'

Sleep. . .

No such thing in a busy hospital. Gina's breakfast arrived almost as soon as Wayne left and she was amazed to discover how hungry she was. She ate cornflakes, two eggs and bacon, three pieces of toast and looked around for more. As she regretfully drained the last of her coffee two policemen arrived, one the sergeant who had helped lift her from the cliff the night before and a younger constable with pen and pad poised.

Contrary to what Wayne had said, they made not the slightest suggestion that she was in any way responsible. They keep their questions brief and to the point.

'You know we have him?' they told her as the questioning ceased and the constable folded his pad.

'Mick. . .?'

'Mick spent an exceedingly uncomfortable night,' the sergeant said in satisfaction. 'Finally came out into the lower paddock this morning and we got him. Ripped himself on some barbed wire trying to get away, too. Your Dr Maitland is stitching him now.'

'I've finished stitching.' It was Struan again, striding into the ward behind the policemen. 'He's all finished, boys. Take him away and find some cold, hard little cell for him. Preferably with a draught.'

'I'm sorry we had to bring him here to be stitched,' the policeman told Struan. 'To have to treat him after what he's done. . .'

'Think nothing of it,' Struan said blandly. 'I enjoyed it.'

'Enjoyed?' It was Gina from the bed, her eyes wide. 'Enjoyed. . .'

'Well, I had to give him some local anaesthetic for the stitching, of course.' Struan grinned. 'I could have been up before the medical board if I didn't. Luckily, though, we had a probationary nurse in today. She's never given an injection and everyone has to start some time. So today was her big chance.'

The sister had come in behind Struan. Her eyes were dancing. 'He made poor Annie give the lot,' she told them. 'Annie was scared stiff before she started and our patient was so unkind as to swear at her. Violently. It made poor Annie's hand shake, and then——' she gave a tiny chuckle '—then Dr Maitland decided we'd best give him a tetanus booster—immunoglobulin *and* tet toxin—and, of course, two million units of penicillin in case of infection.'

'Of course, penicillin,' Struan interjected. 'I'd have been negligent if we didn't give it to him.'

'Give it to him's right,' Sister twinkled. 'The penicillin had to go into his backside and Annie nearly died. He has a huge dragon tattooed on his buttock, and Dr Maitland told her to give the dragon another eye. The way Annie's hand shook she nearly gave him five eyes.'

'You can't be too careful,' Struan said blandly. 'I'd hate to be sued for negligence by missing a necessary injection. He seems to be feeling a bit seedy at the moment, though, even after Annie's and my best efforts. I'd keep him on clear fluids for the rest of the day.'

'If you say so, Doc.' The policeman grinned. 'It'll be our pleasure.'

He and his companion left, bustled out by the sister, who clearly wanted the unsavoury Mick out of her sanitised hospital. Gina and Struan were left alone.

'That. . .that wasn't exactly ethical,' Gina managed, and Struan shook his head.

'Entirely ethical, Dr Buchanan. And I'm your boss now. You have to agree.' He crossed to her bedside and drew the cover up to her chin. His fingers were light against her shoulders, but the touch made her tremble.

'Cold, Dr Buchanan?' There was tenderness in his eyes.

'N-no.'

'Then I suggest you sleep. The more you rest, the faster you'll be fit to come on to my staff. And I'll admit I'm looking forward to the prospect.'

'You don't have to employ me,' Gina managed. 'I. . .I don't want anyone to feel sorry for me.'

'I don't feel at all sorry for you,' Struan told her. His fingers moved upward to touch the dressing on her forehead. 'You kept your cool in a situation where most people I know would be a mass of hysterics. You were badly injured but kept your head enough to attend Lloyd. You coped with my anger. No matter how grateful you might be to us, the fact remains that your cool head saved both of us as well. You killed the dog and you stopped Lloyd bleeding to death. You're very welcome on my staff, Dr Buchanan.'

'I. . .' Words wouldn't come. 'Thank. . .thank you.'

'Don't thank me.' His eyes narrowed with laughter. 'There's another reason you'd best recover fast. It's against all medical ethics to proposition a patient, and if you knew just how beautiful you are. . .' He took

a deep breath and his eyes told her his words were
sincere. His fingers traced the contours of her face.
'Well, enough for now,' he added softly. 'Just recover
fast. And then. . . Well, the worthy Wayne might
find that for once in his honourable life he has some
opposition.'

CHAPTER THREE

STRUAN didn't come near her after that, which was just as well. Gina's mind went into a near-panic every time someone mentioned his name.

'He's off duty,' the nurses told her on Saturday afternoon. 'He's flying down to Melbourne to see Lloyd, and he's staying overnight.'

Of course. He would. Gina remembered the compassion in those eyes and the tenderness of his touch and knew that the fate of someone he employed would be a big responsibility. He really cared.

The news from Melbourne was subdued. There was still no movement. The fracture was stable, though, and there was a little feeling, so maybe. . .

A tiny prayer drifted round and round in Gina's head every waking moment. The thought of Lloyd becoming a paraplegic because of his actions on her behalf was almost more than she could bear.

'It's not all your fault,' Wayne told her. 'He was a damned fool to go near the bikers.'

'He just came for a ride up the mountain to look over the sea,' Gina told him. 'And when he saw what was happening he came in. If he hadn't. . .'

'He rides a bike, though, doesn't he?' Wayne demanded—the ultimate disapproval.

'Oh, Wayne. . .'

Gina lay back on her pillows and let the events of Friday night drift. So much to think about. . .

On Sunday afternoon the doctor on duty let her up. Lesley Marne was a doctor in her fifties, tall and thin, with grey hair caught up in a bun and matching eyes that laughed all the time. She inspected Gina's leg and nodded with approval.

'If we leave you lying here much longer you'll atrophy,' she told her. 'A slow walk around the hospital on crutches, I think.'

She accompanied Gina on the tour, pointing out the features of the small hospital with obvious pride.

'There are five doctors in the town,' she told Gina. 'We all have hospital rights, although we're all in private practice. Except Lloyd, of course. With a resident here full-time we have someone to cope in an emergency until one of us can get here. Two of the rest of us are always on call-back duty.'

'It sounds a bit risky.' Gina was used to city hospitals, where a full medical team was constantly present.

'Most private hospitals don't even have that,' Lesley told her. 'Struan has fought hard to have a training resident based here. That's why. . .'

'Why it's important for me to fill in for him.' Gina nodded.

'You don't mind?'

'No,' Gina admitted honestly. She was having trouble concentrating on her crutches. 'As well as helping Lloyd out, this'll give me a good chance to get to know the hospital and the people before I take up private practice.'

'And you'll take part in the roster for the hospital when you do start private practice?' Lesley grinned. 'You haven't much choice, I'm afraid. If you want to admit patients here you have to be part of the team. The alternative is sending your patients to the city—something the patients themselves will resent.'

She swung open the door of the children's ward as she spoke, and Struan Maitland looked up from the bed of a small patient.

'Struan,' Lesley exclaimed. 'I didn't know you were back from Melbourne.'

'I arrived ten minutes ago.' Struan's smile was etched with exhaustion. A harrowing weekend, then. He turned away and picked up the hand of the child in the bed. 'And I came straight in to see my favourite girl.'

Gina looked down to see an elfin-like little girl lying back on the pillows. Her dark eyes were huge in a tiny face, and shadows spoke of unknown terrors. The paediatrician in Gina started asking questions. Something was badly wrong here.

'You needn't have worried. We've looked after your Lisa.' Lesley smiled down at the little girl. 'You tell Dr Maitland we've done all the right things.'

The child didn't speak. She looked up but her eyes were empty of all expression. Her hand was limp in Struan's grasp.

'This is Dr Buchanan,' Struan told Lisa. He smiled across at Gina. 'She doesn't look like a doctor, though, does she?' In her nightgown and on crutches Gina didn't look anything of the sort. 'She's had an accident,' Struan added.

The child said nothing. It was doubtful she even heard. Her eyes were watchful but expressionless. Nothing, but nothing, was going to interest her. Her huge eyes spoke the message clearly.

'Lisa's been eating,' Lesley told Struan. She sighed. 'At least we're over that hurdle.'

'Hey, Lisa. . .' Struan rumpled the child's tousled brown curls and stood up. 'That's great news. And here's Sister with something else. Sausages, I'd say, by the smell. My favourite.'

No answer. Nothing. The child didn't move. Gina watched as the nurse moved the apathetic Lisa into sitting position and started feeding her. Lisa's mouth opened and she chewed obediently—blind obedience.

The child seemed in shock. . .

Gina moved awkwardly to the end of the bed and glanced down at the chart. The top sheet was for the last three days. No change in temp or blood pressure. What. . .?

'I think we can leave you to your meal, Lisa,' Struan was saying. 'I'll see you in the morning.'

The child didn't look up.

The three doctors moved out into the corridor. Struan held the door for Lesley and waited patiently for Gina to hobble through.

'Nice to see you back on your feet, Dr Buchanan.'

Gina flashed him a look and then smiled. 'Only just.'

'You haven't had Lisa up, have you?' Struan asked, and Lesley shook her head.

'No. We tried again yesterday and today. She falls. There's nothing there.' She sighed. 'I think another couple of days and we'll have to send her to Melbourne, Struan.'

'What's wrong?' Gina looked from Struan to Lesley, and knew from their faces that it wasn't a nice story.

'Lisa's mum was single,' Struan said shortly. 'Lisa's an only child. Her mum committed suicide last week and Lisa. . . Well, Lisa was with her for two days before she was found.'

Silence. Horror kept at bay for twenty years slammed back with a vengeance.

Gina had blocked out the memory of the night her mother died—the blind panic and then stoic acceptance as she had waited for the world to find her. Now, though. . . She had only had to wait until morning. To have waited for two long days. . .

Struan stepped forward as her face drained of colour.

'Dr Buchanan. . .' His hands gripped her and his dark eyes flashed concern. 'Are you all right?'

Lesley's face creased in worry. 'It's Gina's first time up, Struan. Maybe we've done a bit much.'

'Then, let's get you back to bed.' Without waiting

for agreement Struan swept Gina up into his arms, striding swiftly down the hospital corridor to her room.

'Put. . .put me down.'

'You'll fall down if I do,' Struan retorted.

'I won't. . .'

'You won't be given the chance.' Struan pushed open the door of Gina's room with his foot and his eyes gleamed down at her. 'Allow yourself to be cherished, Gina Buchanan. You'd better get used to it.'

'Why? What. . .?'

'Well, you are going to marry Wayne, aren't you?' His eyes twinkled mischief. 'Cherish you to death, our Wayne, I reckon. That is, unless it clashes with his chess ambition.' He laid her down on the bed and stood back. His gaze ran over her speculatively and he moved to the end of the bed to pick up her chart. 'You're still white as a sheet. Is that due to exhaustion, Dr Buchanan? Or was it what we said about Lisa?'

Gina closed her eyes. 'It's bad,' she admitted. 'Lisa. . .'

'It is.' He grimaced. 'About as bad as it can get. We should transfer her to the psychiatric unit of the children's hospital, but. . .'

'But?'

'But Lisa's only living relative is her mother's sister, Sandra. At the moment she's visiting Lisa for five minutes once a day—a perfunctory visit, you might say, but still a visit. If we move her, Lisa won't even have that—and Aunty Sandra will wash her hands of the child entirely. Out of sight, out of mind. So Lisa will have to cope with an institution or foster care. . .'

'Adoption?'

'Maybe. . . But by the time they locate the father and organise the red tape Lisa will be a teenager. She'll be a case for short-term foster care until then, and frankly I don't want her to go that road. If I can help her build up a relationship with the aunt. . .'

'You can't create what's not there.'

'I know. But if I move her now then I don't give it a chance.'

Gina was silent. The shadowed face of Lisa stayed with her. Gina had been older. . .

'She hasn't talked since we found her,' Struan was saying. 'There's been nothing.' He looked down at Gina, his eyes narrowing speculatively. 'But we have a paediatrician on staff now. Maybe. . .'

'I'm not a psychiatrist.'

'No. But you care, Dr Buchanan.' A weary smile lit his face. 'And that'll have to do.'

Speaking of caring. . . 'How. . .how was Lloyd?' Gina asked.

Lesley had come in behind them. She was propping Gina's crutches against the wall but listening at the same time. Her face mirrored Gina's concern.

'Better than I thought.' Struan's face lightened for a moment. 'There's definite feeling. He's immobile, of course—fully tractioned—and it'll be six weeks or so before the swelling subsides enough for the full extent of the damage to be known, but the signs are that he'll recover at least some movement.'

Thank you. . . The prayer inside Gina halted for just a moment and then kept right on going. Good. Make it better. . .

'And you?' He smiled down at her and then looked across at Lesley. 'What are we going to do with this patient, Doctor?'

'If she was mine I might discharge her,' Lesley said cautiously. 'If she had somewhere to go to. Are you planning on moving in with Wayne?'

'Heaven forbid.' Struan didn't give Gina a chance to answer. 'This is a small town, Dr Buchanan, and small towns hold their morality dear. You don't intend shocking their socks off, do you?'

Gina frowned. Wayne was renting a house near the

hospital and it did have a spare room. It seemed sensible. . .

'If she's acting resident then she really needs to live in,' Lesley said thoughtfully. 'And the residence is vacant.'

'My thoughts exactly.'

Whatever Lesley and Struan were talking about, Gina wasn't in on it, and she wasn't enjoying the sensation.

'I'm not taking Lloyd's rooms,' she said stiffly, and Lesley laughed.

'We wouldn't suggest it. Lloyd has a music system that takes up a room and a half. He sleeps somehow, squashed into what's left. There's another flat, though—designed as nurses' accommodation before nurses got so all-fired independent.'

Gina bit her lip. 'I'd have to talk to Wayne. . .' The thought of her own flat was appealing, though. A bit more time, her treacherous heart was saying. A little more freedom before. . .

'You really haven't much choice,' Struan told her. 'If you want the job. . . Do you want the job?'

Gina sighed and nodded. It was out of her hands. Her whole life at the moment, it seemed, was out of her hands.

'Fine, then.' A busy man with one job accomplished. 'We'll move you in tomorrow morning.'

'Wayne can move me in.'

'Oh, of course,' Struan said blandly. 'I'd forgotten Wayne.'

This wasn't going to work. Gina lay back as peace settled over the hospital and tried to make herself think.

She was being bulldozed. Struan Maitland moved through the place like a whirlwind, moving all before him. Even the other doctors were deferential.

'He's not so special,' she told herself crossly, shifting

in bed. Her thigh was aching with a dull grind after
the walk. It was going to be a week before she was
useful around the place. A week. . .

She glanced at her watch. Wayne had said he'd come
in tonight. Wayne. . .

She tried to conjure the warmth Wayne's presence
had always engendered, but tonight it wasn't even to
be remembered.

Damn Struan Maitland.

It was just that the man was so darned big. Size. . .
That was all it was.

It had nothing to do with size. It had everything to
do with the way his eyes looked straight into her.
Straight to her heart.

For heaven's sake, Gina. Get a grip on yourself.
Remember the old vow, Gina Buchanan, and get on
with your life.

It was funny how vows were made to be broken. If
Gina had really meant what she'd vowed she would
have stayed firmly in her hospital bed. Instead, she
found herself too restless to settle after an early tea,
and her crutches beckoned. Her crutches and Lisa. . .

She made her way painfully down the corridor. The
nurse looked up as Gina entered the children's ward,
smiled and put her hand to her lips in a signal to be
quiet. Lisa was the only patient in the room, and Lisa
was asleep.

Or was she? Gina crossed to the bed and stood
looking down at the pathetic little bundle under the
bedclothes. Lisa's eyes were closed, but it was as if
she was willing them to stay closed. On impulse Gina
sat down beside the bed. Her hand went out and she
touched the curls. Softly. She ran her fingers through
and through the child's hair—a feather-touch of
reassurance to a child who desperately sought sleep.

Lisa's eyelids flickered once—just once—as though

checking out a fearful hope. There was blank misery as she saw who was touching her and the eyes closed again.

'I know,' Gina whispered down to the child. 'I'm not your mum, Lisa. I know how you feel, though. My mum died when I was not much more than your age, and I thought it was the end of the world. I thought I was going to be by myself forever. I wasn't, though, Lisa. I found there were people who were still mine. Friends. People who I still needed and who needed me.' Her voice wasn't much more than a whisper as she stroked the little girl's hair. 'I'm pretty much alone now, though, Lisa. I've only just come to Gundowring and I've hurt myself. I guess. . .I guess I could use a friend almost as much as you could.'

There wasn't an answer. Gina hadn't expected one. She didn't move, though.

She sat for close on an hour, her thigh aching with the enforced stillness. Her hand never stopped.

And gradually, gradually, she had the satisfaction of seeing the tension ease out of the little face, and Lisa drifted into natural, unfeigned sleep.

She'd achieved the child a peaceful night, she thought as she finally ceased her stroking. For now, it was all she could ask.

She turned from the bed to find Wayne watching from the door.

Wayne. . .

She stood, fumbling for her crutches, her eyes lighting in a smile. 'Wayne. . .I'm glad you came. Sorry I wasn't in my ward.'

'They told me you were here.' Wayne frowned across at the sleeping Lisa. 'I don't think they should have you working yet.'

'They don't.' She received his perfunctory kiss. 'I just. . . She's so alone, Wayne. . .'

'Yeah.' Wayne's eyes softened a little. 'Like you used to be. And it looks as if she'll end up in foster-care too.'

Gina bit her lip. Her eyes went to the sleeping child and a knot of misery welled up inside her. A lonely, lonely road. . .

There was a flurry of activity at the desk and a big blonde woman with a harried expression came down the corridor towards them. Gina was blocking the door.

'Can I get in, please. . .?' The woman was clearly in a hurry.

'Lisa's just gone to sleep,' Gina said gently. 'Are you. . .are you her aunt?'

'Yeah.' The woman looked Gina up and down in suspicion. 'What's it to you?'

'I'm Gina Buchanan.' With difficulty she held out her hand and took the woman's. It was hard not to wobble at the same time. 'I know I don't look like it, but I'm a paediatrician. Dr Maitland asked me to see Lisa.'

'Oh. . .' The woman's eyes widened and she grinned. 'Oh, I know. I've heard about you. The whole town's been talking. . .' She flashed a look at Wayne, as though she had trouble connecting he and Gina, and then motioned down to the bag she was carrying. 'I'm not waking Lisa. I just brought her a change of nightie.'

'It wouldn't hurt to wake her.' If Lisa hadn't seen her aunt all day it would do her good to have a visitor. More good than sleep. . . Gina could get her back to sleep again later.

'No.' The woman backed off. 'I'm not staying. The kids haven't had their tea yet. We spent today on the beach. I have all the school clothes to iron before morning. . .'

'How many children do you have?' Beside her Gina

could sense Wayne growing restless. She blocked it out.

'Three.' Sandra's voice was suddenly defensive. 'And three's enough. I know they reckon I should have Lisa, but I'm damned if I will. My old man was mad enough when I wanted to have a third kid. We have three girls already. It might be different if Lisa was a boy—but even then. . . No. She's my sister's kid—and if Jenny was selfish enough to kill herself she's not bloody saddling me with the kid.' She shoved the bag at Gina—nearly knocking her over in the process—and turned to stalk out of the hospital.

'Whew. . .' Wayne watched her thoughtfully, and then turned back to relieve Gina of the laundry bag. 'I reckon the kid'd be better off in foster-care than with that one.'

'She might,' Gina said non-committally. She didn't believe it for a moment.

The little flat beside the hospital was fully furnished and very comfortable. Gina spent most of Monday in hospital, but after work Wayne came and took her through to her new home.

She sat and looked out of the window at the sea while Wayne unpacked for her.

'You travel light,' he said approvingly. 'Apart from your books you hardly own a thing.'

'No.' She never had. Moving from home to home there had been no way she could collect possessions and she'd got out of the habit.

'Tell you what,' Wayne suggested, 'if you're up to it, Gina, I'll run you up to show you the house I have my eye on. The I'll take you out to dinner. There's a good little restaurant down on the waterfront that's not too expensive.'

Not too expensive. . .

It hadn't taken Gina long to realise that Wayne

watched every cent he earned. The day after she'd arrived in hospital he'd come with an apology instead of flowers.

'They wanted twenty dollars for one posy!' he'd exclaimed in horror. 'And it won't last more than a few days.'

Gina looked down at the third finger of her left hand. There was nothing there as yet. She wondered just what Wayne intended putting there.

She forced herself to concentrate on what Wayne was saying. See the house. . . Dinner. . .

'I'd like that.'

The house was almost exactly what Gina had imagined. It was a triple-fronted brick veneer in a row of homes that looked almost identical. A nice, suburban house. . .

This was what she wanted, she reminded herself bleakly. All the time she had been growing up she had so longed for security. Wayne was the only one who had offered it.

And now she had it. An administrator for a husband—a kind, considerate husband, who would never put her at risk. A home like everyone else. . .

'I'm trying to push their price down,' Wayne was saying. 'If they'll drop another five thousand we'll have it.'

'You mean. . .you mean, you gave them an offer before you knew whether I'd like it?'

Wayne frowned. 'I knew you'd like it. It's a sensible house.'

'I know it's a sensible house. . .'

The house fitted Wayne like a glove. Gina could see him out mowing the lawns every Sunday, washing the car. . .

What on earth was wrong with her? This was what she wanted. This was what she had ached for from childhood—wasn't it?

Wayne drove down the street to the the Steak Supreme. It was a glorious night but the doors on the small restaurant shut it out with a bang. There were low ceilings, lower lights, and waiters who were obsequious to a fault. Wayne loved it.

'And it's not even expensive,' he told Gina as the waiter disappeared with their order.

'I can't understand why not.' Gina looked at the badly painted mural of Southern France on the wall and tried to imagine what the view would be if they knocked a wall out right there. Harbour lights and the beckoning sea. . .

The meal justified the prices and Gina grew more and more depressed. Wayne appeared not to notice, but as they stood to leave he handed her the crutches and smiled down at her.

'It's been a bit much. I can tell your leg's hurting.'

'Yes. . .'

It hadn't been hurting in the least.

'I'll take you home straight away.'

'I'd like that.' She flashed a grateful glance up at him and winced. This, then, was how it would be. Proprietorial Wayne and grateful Gina.

Wayne drove her slowly back to the hospital, mindful of her hip. He turned the corners with such care that Gina was almost ready to scream. For heaven's sake. . .

'I won't come in,' he told her as they finally reached their destination. 'I know you need your sleep.' He looked at her, his blue eyes anxious. 'We haven't done too much? You enjoyed yourself?'

'I haven't done too much,' Gina assured him. Too much. . . She was almost asleep with excitement!

'Goodnight, then, my love.' He leaned her crutches on the car, took her hands in his and gently kissed her.

It was the same kiss she had experienced aged eight.

'Kiss Gina goodbye,' his mother had told him, and

Wayne had dutifully obliged. Usually Gina had clung.
The kiss had meant the beginning of another dreary
month with no contact with her past.

That was all it had meant, though, and surely
now. . . Surely it should mean something more?

She was passive, and Wayne expected nothing else
of her. Indeed, she thought, he'd be shocked. Nice
girls didn't kiss. . . Nice girls lay back and thought of
England. . .

Oh, for heaven's sake, Gina, you're never going to
make a marriage thinking like this. She pulled back
from Wayne and her eyes were troubled.

He noticed nothing.

'Take care.' He smiled and patted her with avuncular
affection on the arm. He climbed back into his sensible
sedan and motored sedately off.

'Thus ends a night of passion.'

Gina whirled. Struan Maitland had come out of the
hospital entrance and was standing in the shadows—
watching. 'I always wondered how the man would kiss,'
he said conversationally. 'And now I know.'

Gina flushed to the roots of her hair. Her crutches
wobbled dangerously. Speechless didn't adequately
describe her emotions.

'You know, in my book a gentleman doesn't let the
lady of his dreams struggle to the door on crutches.'
Struan came towards her down the darkened path.
'Especially when the path's rough and covered with
dangerous obstacles.'

Gina's breath quickened. 'The only obstacle in my
way is you,' she managed.

'And would you say I'm dangerous?' Polite enquiry.

'Of course not.' And that was a lie, if ever she'd
uttered one. He was dangerous for all sorts of reasons,
not the least being what his presence was doing to her
pulse-rate.

'Does he always kiss you like that?' Once more,

enquiry only. Nothing more. Struan fell into slow step beside her and when she reached the door took the key and slid it into the lock. Undoubtedly his presence made things easier. Why, then, did she want him to go away?

'It's none of your business how my fiancé kisses me.'

'No.' He flicked on the light and looked around. 'Nice and homey,' he said approvingly. 'Of course, it always was. You don't have many possessions, Dr Buchanan, or are they coming?'

'This is all I have.' Gina crossed to the stool by the kitchen bench and sank down. Once seated she felt more on her own terms. If only the man would shrink a bit. . .

'Not even an engagement ring?' He crossed to where she sat and lifted her hand. 'Don't tell me—our Wayne thinks it's much more sensible to put the money into bricks and mortar.'

'Our relationship is none of your business.' Gina snatched her hand away, her face still burning.

'No.' His eyes gleamed down at her. 'Except that you're my patient, and what I see in your eyes tells me you and Wayne are as suited to each other as Little Red Riding Hood and the wolf.'

Gina bit her lip. 'Wayne's no wolf,' she said stiffly.

'No.' He grinned. 'I didn't think he was the one with passion in his soul. . . It'll have to be our Wayne who's Little Red, then.'

'Look, just because he's an administrator and he wears a suit. . .'

'And adds up how much every last teabag in this place costs, and throws it at me if I let my elderly patients have second cups. It's OK if they recycle, but heaven help them if they want their second cup strong. He insists on the cheapest caterers' blend coffee, and then I find that his own office is equipped with best Colombian—and a coffee-plunger. He doesn't back me up one inch in my fights for funding with the health commission—in fact he's behind half their damned cost-cutting measures. The man has a parsimonious soul, Dr Buchanan.'

'Look, this is nothing to do with me. . .'

'Oh, but it is.' He nodded slowly. 'I'm just telling you that when you marry him you'll be recycling tea-bags and having real cream on every second Sunday of the month and. . .'

'Will you just shut up?' Gina was half laughing, half-serious. 'Dr Maitland, who I choose to marry— and why—is nothing to do with you. Your concern is touching, but I don't need it.'

'So you've set your heart absolutely on marriage?'

'Yes!' She almost yelled it at him.

'Why?' The question was bland as milk.

'Because. . .' She shouldn't have answered him. The question had been going round and round her head all day, driving her nuts. 'Because I want to be settled. I want to have a home and a husband and babies. I want. . .'

'Is that all?' He cut her short and she glared at him.

'That's enough. I want to be married.'

'So marry me.'

She gasped. Her mouth sagged. Struan Maitland stood before her, blackbearded and dangerous, and his eyes were only half laughing.

'You have. . .you have got to be joking.'

'Never more serious.' The laughter suddenly died out of his eyes and his hand came up to touch the dressing on her face. 'Maybe it's time I did a bit of settling down. A spot of cherishing. . .'

'Struan Maitland, I would never marry you.'

'Why not?' He sounded, of all things, injured.

'Because. . .' She looked helplessly up at him, wishing she were big enough to throw him forcibly out of the door. And his eyes caught hers and held.

The laughter died. There was a deathly hush in the room. Everything was still. It seemed that even her heart had stopped.

'Because you're dangerous,' Gina whispered. 'You represent everything I most dislike in men. You stand there with your great bearded face. . .'

'You don't like my beard?' Wounded dignity.

'No, I don't like your beard!'

'Is that all?'

'No, it's not all. . .'

'But my beard is definitely a factor?' He was laughing at her again, and Gina was lost in the warmth of that laughter.

'Yes. No.' Good grief, she was making no sense at all. 'Struan Maitland, get out of my flat. I'm marrying Wayne, and that's all there is to it.'

He shook his head. 'No,' he smiled. 'That's not all there is to it, my beautiful Gina. The siege has hardly begun.'

CHAPTER FOUR

LEFT to her own devices, Gina slept until late morning. She rose, showered and breakfasted, and then decided on a visit to Lisa. She'd gone one step out of her flat before she heard the news.

The beard was gone

'You should see him,' one of the junior nurses told her breathlessly. 'I always thought men grew beards because they didn't have a chin, or something. But Dr Maitland. . . Oh, Dr Buchanan. . .you should see him. He's gorgeous!

Gina stopped dead. She'd been limping down the corridor and now. . .

Gina ran last night's conversation back through her head and found her crutches wobbling of their own accord.

For heaven's sake. . . The man was setting her up. Baiting her. . . If he wanted to shave off his beard it had absolutely nothing to do with her.

She made her way unsteadily to the children's ward and was told by no less than four other people on the way.

'Maybe he just got tired of it?' the children's ward sister suggested. 'It was a great beard, but, boy—when you see what's underneath you wonder why he was hiding it.'

At least the man had been and gone. He'd done his round early and was now safely ensconced in his consulting-rooms. . . Consulting, Gina hoped. Please. . . Long may you consult, Struan Maitland.

Lisa was staring straight up to the ceiling. She didn't look around as Gina came in.

Gina had discarded the nightwear she had worn in hospital, her ordinary clothes making her feel heaps better. Jeans were hard to get over her hip so she'd chosen a flowing skirt and light blouse. Deliberately, she'd made it gay. Her skirt was covered with pale lemon polka dots, and she was wearing loopy gold earrings, the sort of outfit that should appeal to a five-year-old. . . She sat on the bed and smiled down at Lisa.

'Do I look a little more like a doctor this morning, Lisa?'

No answer. The child didn't show by a flicker of her eyelids that she'd heard.

Gina sat and stroked the child's hair and thought. Finally she beckoned to the charge nurse.

'Sister, can you find me a wheelchair?'

The nurse looked doubtfully at Lisa. 'She won't sit up, Dr Buchanan. We could strap her in, but. . .' She looked doubtfully at Gina's crutches. 'How on earth. . .?'

'I don't intend to push.' Gina smiled. 'It'd be the blind leading the blind if I did. I'd really like to sit out in the sun, though. It's a lovely morning. I thought if you put me in a wheelchair and I held Lisa on my lap we could both go.'

The nurse looked doubtfully from Lisa to Gina and back again. 'If you think it will do some good, Doctor. . .'

'I don't think anything,' Gina told her. 'I just hope.' She took a deep breath. 'Let's get Lisa dressed too, shall we? Does she have a dress?'

Between the hospital and the sea, gardens had been laid out with care. Three elderly residents of the nursing home looked up from their gardening labours and greeted Gina before they got back to work. Nice, Gina thought. If they had to move into a nursing home then it was great that they could make it theirs.

'I wouldn't stay in the wheelchair, Doc,' one of the men called out. The whole town knew who Gina was by now. They had taken her to their hearts. That such a thing could happen to a new, young doctor in their town. . . 'There's a cane lounger around the back. Charlie and me will haul it round for you.'

She wasn't allowed to protest. Five minutes later she and Lisa were settled on a comfortable padded lounger in a sheltered nook, propped up with pillows and with a blanket placed tenderly over their legs.

'Hey, I'm supposed to be the doctor,' Gina grinned. 'And you're supposed to be the patients.'

'Huh!' The woman placing the blanket over Gina's legs was ninety if she was a day, and she gave a scornful laugh. 'If you young things get yourselves into trouble then it's always the older generation that has to cope.'

The woman looked down at Lisa, cradled in Gina's arms. 'And if you can do something for the bairn. . .' she said softly, and then moved away.

Gina was left to lie in peace, looking out over the distant sea and cradling the passive Lisa.

She asked nothing of the child. Her arm rested around her, and her free hand lightly stroked her head, but she made no demands. It was enough to let the sun filter down through the huge, overhanging gum trees, warming their faces—doing its own healing.

The morning slowly passed. Gina didn't move. She didn't want to. Her thigh was still a swollen mess and she knew her body needed rest more than anything. She drifted in and out of sleep, aware that the child beside her did the same. Gina had been physically hurt, but Lisa's wounds were deeper.

Gina stirred at about lunch-time, and looked down to find Lisa's eyes wide. Her tiny body was rigid.

'What's the matter, my Lisa?'

There was no answer. Gina knew what the problem

was, though. She was aware of it herself. They'd had a long drink two hours ago and there was a pressing need.

Gina didn't move. The child was nestled against her, cradled against the pretty yellow and white skirt.

A problem. . . And Gina wanted Lisa to work it out for herself.

Lisa had been incontinent in bed. Passively incontinent. The nurses had taken to putting large nappies on her, but before they'd come outside Gina had shaken her head when the nurse had started to put one on her.

Now. . . Now Lisa needed urgently to empty her bladder, and she was lying on Gina's skirt.

Gina said nothing. She willed lunch not to arrive. Not yet. A few more moments and Lisa was going to have to make a decision.

The child writhed in discomfort and Gina's arm tightened. 'It's OK, Lisa,' she said calmly. 'I won't let you fall. Our lunch will come soon. I'm hungry, aren't you?'

Silence. Gina could feel the child's body, rigid with tension.

Please. . . Please. . . Let this work.

'Hey! My two favourite ladies in the whole world. . .' Gina looked up to see Struan striding across the grass towards them.

Without his beard. . .

The wind whipped his dark hair. His face was lean and aquiline, his mouth wide and strong. Impossibly handsome. . . In his classic tailored trousers and open-necked shirt, with the breeze ruffling the strong hairs at his throat, he looked a million dollars. Gina stared up at him in stunned silence as Struan stooped over Lisa.

'Recognise me, young lady?' he smiled down at the child. 'Dr Buchanan reckoned my beard was enough

to scare off potential brides. Well, one potential bride.
So it had to go. . .' He moved to lift the child from
Gina, but Gina gave a fast, urgent shake of her head.
The tension was growing.

Silence.

Struan stood, looking down at them, and Gina
blessed him for his sensitivity. If it had been anyone
else. . .

The child was stiff with holding back. Gina didn't
move. The yellow and white skirt floated around and
under them. Decision. . .

'Toilet. . .' Lisa whispered.

Struan's eyes widened, but Gina shook her head
once more. She bent towards Lisa. 'Sorry, Lisa, what
did you say?'

'Toilet. . .' It was an urgent cry, and it was as much
as Gina could do not to weep with relief. Lisa's first
word. A start. . .

She looked up to Struan and his grin was as wide
as hers.

'Dr Maitland, Lisa needs to go to the toilet,' Gina
told him, managing to keep her voice even and matter-
of-fact. 'Could you oblige?'

'It would be my very great pleasure.' Struan scooped
the child into his arms and smiled down at her. 'Well
done, Lisa, love. . .'

It wasn't quite. The five-year-old had waited a bit
too long. A lot too long. . . The movement as Struan
jolted her and the relief of being at last clear of Dr
Buchanan's pretty skirt was enough. The child's bladder emptied involuntarily and Lisa's eyes widened with
dismay. Her face crumpled and a couple of tears rolled
down her cheeks.

Tears. . . There had been nothing. No sign of emo-
tion. And now. . . Gina's smile broadened, and even
Struan's smile didn't slip. A wide, wet stain crept across
the front of his trousers.

'No problem, Lisa, love.' He gave her a hard hug. 'I've ten more pairs of trousers, specially for such occasions. And you saved Dr Buchanan's lovely skirt.' He grinned down at it. 'Washable, is it, Dr Buchanan?'

'Drip-dry,' Gina grinned impishly back. Struan's trousers were a wool mix—dry-clean only, by the look of them. What a shame. . .

A nurse approached, and hesitated as she saw the little group. Struan turned to her and smiled. 'Sister, Lisa needs a change of clothes. Can you oblige?'

'Of course.' The girl smiled at Lisa and made to lift her from Struan's arms. Gina shook her head.

'Wait. . .'

Silence. Was it too soon?

'Lisa, I'm having lunch out here,' she told the little girl. 'Do you want to eat by yourself in the ward or would you like to come back here and eat with me?'

'A picnic,' Struan said approvingly. 'Can I come?'

'If you're good.' Gina glared at him.

'I'm always good.' His voice adopted the injured tone Gina was beginning to know. 'Aren't I, Lisa?'

His eyes laughed down at the child in his arms, and for a fleeting second—so fast that Gina might have imagined it—a trace of a smile lit the depths of the child's unhappiness.

'Will you come back to us, Lisa?' Gina asked.

A long, long silence. Lisa's eyes held Gina's, and then she slowly, slowly turned to look up at Struan. His eyes held laughter, reassurance, and the promise of good things to come. . .

'Yes, please. . .'

'I knew I was right about you.' Struan hauled up a chair beside Gina's lounger as soon as the nurse bore Lisa off. 'Well done, Dr Buchanan.'

Gina eyed him doubtfully. He looked like a man settling in for a long haul.

'She wanted to talk,' Gina told him. 'She just. . .she

just didn't know how. Her life is so out of control. . .'

Gina knew. The nightmare, and then the refusal to keep going. To keep going—to act normally—was to admit that things had irrevocably changed. Her mother's life had ended and so should the world. Stop the world, I want to get off. I can't keep going. . .

Struan was watching her strangely. His eyes were on the shadows under her eyes.

'Want to tell me about it, Dr Buchanan?'

Gina jolted herself back to the present. 'Tell you. . .? Tell you about what?'

'There's shadows. . . Problems. . .'

Gina forced a smile. 'No shadows,' she managed. 'But definitely a problem. I've been hanging on as long as Lisa, and if you don't hand me my crutches and help me up, I refuse to answer for the consequences.'

'You want me to carry you?'

'No, thank you,' Gina said with dignity. 'I make it a rule never to be carried by men with stained trousers.' She grinned. 'If I were you, I'd go and change. From this angle it looks like you had the accident.'

A strange meal. . .

Despite the tensions surrounding them, hospital sandwiches had never tasted so good. Struan spread Gina's rug on the grass, and the three of them sprawled in the shade. Struan laid Lisa with her head on his clean trousers and periodically popped pieces of sandwich into her mouth. He made it a game—aeroplanes, like one would play with a toddler—and more than once Gina saw laughter surface.

The child was back in her nightwear and back in her silence. No problem, Gina thought. There was no hurry.

'She only has the one dress,' the nurse told Gina when she brought Lisa back out in her nightie. 'The one she was wearing when she was brought in.'

Gina nodded.

'We need to get you some clothes,' she said thoughtfully as she held a cup for Lisa to drink. 'Now you're getting better.'

'What about going out to Lisa's house tonight and collecting them?' Struan asked, and Gina thought.

'OK,' she said slowly. 'Lisa can come with us. She can choose what she needs.'

This time there was no mistaking the flash of expression in the child's eyes. Fear. . .

Struan hesitated. 'Too soon, Dr Buchanan?'

'No.' Gina thought of what she had been told. It was over a week since Lisa's mum had died. She had to face it and somehow keep going. Learn that she could. And the longer they waited, the more the fear would grow.

'Well, how about it if I run you and Lisa out to her house tonight after work?' Struan smiled. 'Would you like that, Lisa?'

The child had retreated again. Gina had expected nothing less.

'Not on your motorbike,' Gina said smartly.

'You wouldn't both fit.'

'What a shame. . .'

'Don't you like my motorbike, Dr Buchanan?'

'If I say no, will you get rid of it?'

He met her look. His teasing smile stayed exactly where it was.

'I might,' he admitted. 'Though it's asking a lot for love. . .'

'Dr Maitland!'

'Yes, my love. . .?'

'I am not——' She stopped, breathless. This was running way out of her control. A nurse was approaching from the hospital entrance and Gina looked up gratefully.

'Your receptionist is on the telephone, Dr Maitland,'

the girl said primly. 'She said, have you forgotten that you were supposed to be in Theatre ten minutes ago?'

'Irresponsible bikers,' Gina couldn't resist saying. 'You can't depend on them for anything.'

Struan flashed her a wide, encompassing smile.

'You'll pay for that, Dr Buchanan. But I'm a patient man. I'll bide my time.'

At six that night Struan drove to the hospital in a very sedate hospital car to collect his two passengers. He'd rung from the surgery, so Gina and Lisa were waiting. The nurse had brought Lisa to the hospital entrance in her wheelchair and Gina stood beside her, balancing on her crutches.

She was getting so sick of them. Her arms ached unmercifully and she was itching to wear jeans again. She felt absurdly formal, standing here in her bright skirt. Still. . . Lisa had looked at the skirt as Gina limped out the hospital door and there was no mistaking the flash of satisfaction that had crossed the child's face.

Struan's car pulled up at almost the same time as Wayne emerged from the hospital entrance.

'Hey, Gina. . .' Wayne called, and then saw Struan. His face tightened.

'We're taking Lisa out to fetch some clothes from her house,' Gina said quickly, attempting to deflect the tension she could see bristling across Wayne's face.

'You?' Wayne frowned. He adjusted his tie and came towards the little group. 'Gina, you're supposed to be resting.'

'If I rest any more I'll die of boredom,' Gina smiled. 'And it's hardly a long drive.'

Wayne frowned. He looked down at Lisa. 'It hardly seems appropriate. Can't her aunt bring the kid in some clothes?'

Gina shook her head, trying to keep her voice

light. 'Lisa needs to choose herself, Wayne.' She held Wayne's eyes with an urgent message. 'It's important, Wayne.'

Wayne looked from Gina to Struan and back again. 'Why are you both going?'

'Because I can't drive and I need to be there.' Gina's smile slipped. The last thing she wanted was to have to explain herself before the child.

'I'll drive you, then,' Wayne offered.

'Sorry, mate.' Struan was lifting Lisa into the car while Gina and Wayne talked. 'No can do. My car has insurance for hospital patients being transported. Do you?' His slow smile told Gina that he expected a piece of officialdom was just the thing to hold Wayne at bay.

It worked like a charm. Wayne looked a little mollified.

'All right, then.' He turned back to Gina. 'But I was going to drop in tonight.'

'After chess?' Struan said wickedly, and Wayne flashed him a look of incomprehension.

'As a matter of fact, yes. About eight-thirty, Gina. You'll be back by then, I take it?'

'She might not.' Struan smiled down at Lisa. 'I have plans for a stroll on the beach afterwards. With one patient on crutches and the other in a wheelchair it might take some time.'

'A stroll. . .'

'I've asked the hospital kitchen to provide a picnic tea,' Struan explained calmly. 'And it's a great night for the beach.' His smile widened. 'Tell you what, Wayne, give chess a miss and join us.'

Give chess a miss. . . He had to be joking. Wayne looked from Gina to Struan and back again.

'I'll see you later,' he said shortly, straight at Gina, and stalked off.

'Amorous sort of guy, isn't he?' Struan said blandly, and opened the passenger-side door for Gina.

Gina grimaced. It seemed so hard. 'I should be back for him,' she sighed. 'Now. . . He's disgruntled, to say the least. . .'

Struan grinned, eased himself into the driver's seat and nosed the car out on to the road.

'Seems to me I've never seen the guy gruntled.'

'Gruntled?'

Gina's eyes flew up to Struan's and a bubble of laughter rose. She chuckled, and Struan looked across at her in approval.

'Well, well,' he said slowly, his eyes warm. 'I knew you'd laugh like that, Dr Buchanan. I just knew. I think that's why I decided to marry you.'

Silence. The laughter died. Gina turned to the windscreen and stared straight ahead.

'Don't. . .don't talk nonsense,' she whispered.

'I don't talk nonsense.'

'No?' She took a deep breath. 'You're full of it, Dr Maitland. I'll look up "grunted" in the dictionary when I get home, and prove it to you.'

'Ouch. . .' He winced, but he still smiled. '*Touché*!' He smiled across at her. 'Then, let's just say I don't talk nonsense when I'm serious. And I'm serious now. When I say I intend to marry you.'

'I'm marrying Wayne.' Gina clenched her fingers into her palms. 'And, as I'm not a believer in bigamy, that excludes you, Dr Maitland.'

'Leaves only murder,' Struan said lightly. 'Wayne had better watch his cocoa. . .'

Good grief. . . He had her laughing again. Gina fought back a smile and set her face into wooden disapproval. For heaven's sake. . .

The child in the back seat was absolutely silent. Gina glanced back at her. She was harnessed firmly into position, cushioned by pillows, and her small face was set and tight. Gina gave her a smile, but the child didn't respond.

'We're nearly there, Lisa,' Struan told her, sensing Gina's concern. 'A couple of moments. . .'

The child's face set even tighter.

The laughter died from Gina. For all Struan's levity, life was a serious business. She knew that. The child on the back seat was yet more proof—if she needed it.

She didn't need it. She was set on the right track. She had made her decisions, and she wasn't to be swayed by some damned good-looking male with the most dangerous smile she had ever seen. . .

They pulled off the road a moment later, Struan guiding the car down a rough track leading to a small weatherboard cottage overlooking the sea.

It was a beautiful place. The cottage itself was decrepit, there had been no money to spare here, but the garden was loved. Bright annuals scattered colour in front of the cottage, and further back Gina saw rows and rows of carefully tended vegetables. A garden tended with care. . .

What sort of a woman had Lisa's mother been? A woman who tended her vegetables for a future crop she'd had no intention of living to see? She looked a question up at Struan, but she could tell by his face that he was thinking the same thing.

'It doesn't make any sort of sense,' he muttered. 'And yet. . .'

'The police are certain it was suicide?' Gina asked softly—so softly that the wooden little figure in the back couldn't hear.

'They're sure. Jenny took an overdose of sleeping-pills.'

'Prescribed by. . .?'

He shook his head. 'Not by me.' He frowned again. 'That's another thing that doesn't make sense. The pills. . .'

'So who prescribed them?'

'She must have obtained them in Melbourne.' Struan

grimaced. 'She left Lisa with her sister three weeks ago and spent a day in Melbourne alone. Sandra said she came back depressed. She thinks she might have met Lisa's father again—found out for sure that there was no future with him.'

No future. . . Gina stared out at the welcoming little cottage, and the sea stretching out behind in a wide, bright plane. The waves were cresting just below the house, rushing up to break on the rocks and surge over the sandy beach. Jenny had had a place to live that few could match—and a daughter who loved her. She had had a garden she cared for. . .

'It doesn't make sense. . .'

'Love can do strange things.'

'Not this strange.' Gina set her lips. 'I want to know who prescribed those sleeping-tablets. Has anyone found out?'

'No.' Struan shook his head. 'But it's not important, Gina. She suicided. Is it going to help anyone to investigate the emotional reasons? It's not going to bring her back.'

'No.' Gina's eyes closed in sudden bitter memory. The only thing that had made things bearable. . . She glanced back at Lisa, huddled on the back seat like a limp rag doll. 'It might bring Lisa back, though,' she said softly.

Struan carried Lisa inside. He'd been in the cottage before and knew his way around.

'I came out a few times when Jenny needed house-calls,' Struan explained as he carried the child through into her bedroom. 'When Lisa had tonsillitis and when Jenny fell and hurt her ankle.'

Which made it even stranger that the sleeping-pills had been prescribed by another doctor. Though if she'd been depressed. . . Sometimes depression made patients seek someone who didn't know them—as if their problem was something to be ashamed about.

The small mystery would have to wait. For now, Lisa needed Gina. Her face was deathly pale, and she was limp in Struan's hold.

'Is this your bed, Lisa?' The bright patchwork quilt was drawn up over a carefully made bed. The bedroom was neat and clean, but was obviously a child's bedroom. Bright posters adorned the walls—kittens, horses, alphabet murals. . .

A bedroom cared for by a mum who'd loved her daughter. . .

Gina looked down at the bed. A small, scruffy tiger with a lop-sided grin and one ear missing lay on the coverlet. Gina picked him up as Struan placed the child down, and then nestled it close to Lisa's cheek.

'A friend, Lisa?'

No answer.

'We can take him back to the hospital with us, if you'd like?'

Nothing.

'OK. We'll leave him here. I'll put him out of the way.' Gina's hand moved down again to lift away the little tiger, but she moved slowly, and Lisa moved first. Her hand came up and she clutched the soft toy.

'Sam,' she whispered. Her hand gripped hard and a tear slid down her cheek. 'My Sam. . .'

'You'd like him to come back with us?'

'Yes.'

Gina smiled down at her. So far, so good. 'Well, that's what we're here for, Lisa,' she said gently. She sat on the bed. 'Now, if Dr Maitland will go through your wardrobe, you can tell him what you'd like to take.'

What followed was a very silly half-hour. There were no instructions for what she and Struan were doing in any medical text, Gina thought, and yet they were achieving miracles. The child lay quietly back on her bed, the tension slowly easing from her face as Struan held up one dress after another. Her dressing-gown. Her raincoat. . .

A few inappropriate clothes went into the case, but by the end of it Lisa was almost smiling.

'Will we shut the case now, Lisa?' Struan asked as he folded the last sweater. He lifted his brows in a question to Gina, and Gina nodded. 'Or should we check the rest of the house—just in case we've forgotten something important?'

'That's a good idea,' Gina smiled. 'Would you like to try to walk, Lisa?'

'No.' A scared whisper.

'No worries.' Struan scooped her up into strong arms. 'I'm getting good at this chauffeur business.'

He walked Lisa slowly through the house, chatting to her as they went. Gina hopped along uncomfortably on her crutches behind them.

One room left. Gina took a deep breath and her eyes met Struan's. There was no escaping it. The child had to face this. She turned the knob and pushed the door for Struan to go through.

The bed was stripped, as Struan had told Gina it would be. The room, like Lisa's, was bright and cheerful, with photographs taking the place of Lisa's posters. Photographs of Lisa in every conceivable pose, from birth to now.

Lisa looked around slowly. Gina watched her, but the closed, shuttered face had disappeared. There was pain, but Lisa was moving through it.

'My mum died here,' she whispered.

'She did.' Struan nodded to the bureau, where a framed photograph of a laughing, lovely young woman holding Lisa on her lap stood in a silver frame. 'Would you like to take this back to hospital with you?'

Lisa looked around. 'No,' she said slowly. 'Mummy has a picture of me and Mummy and Frederick. She keeps it in her top drawer.' Her face worked, fighting tears. 'I want one with Mummy and Frederick.'

'I remember Frederick,' Struan nodded. 'Your pony died last year, didn't he?'

'Just like Mummy,' Lisa whispered. Her face crumpled. She pushed against Struan with small fists. 'I want to get down.'

Struan carefully set her on her feet. Lisa gave a gulping sob, walked to the bed on legs that were unsteady from disuse, and crumpled in a tearful, sodden mass on to the mattress.

Struan made an instinctive movement to go to her, but Gina stopped him.

'No, Struan. Let her have her cry out.'

She opened the top drawer of Jenny's bedside cabinet and the photograph Lisa wanted was on the top—a lovely snap of a laughing Lisa and Jenny, with an ancient pony tolerating them both with benign affection. Gina's mouth twisted in a rueful smile. Lisa had had so much. And so had Jenny. . .

She lifted the photograph, and as she did a business card caught her eye—a small slip of white cardboard shoved to the back of the drawer. A doctor's card. Gina lifted it out, then put a hand on Struan's arm as he looked down at the sobbing child. 'I think we should wait outside.'

'Leave her?'

'She has to come to terms with it some time.' Gina crossed and put her hand on Lisa's head. 'Lisa, Dr Maitland and I will be in the garden. Come out when you're ready.' And she pushed Struan out of the door.

'I hope to hell you know what you're doing.' Struan exploded as the door closed behind them. 'If we go back in there and find her in a catatonic state. . .'

Gina shook her head. The sun was low on the horizon, gaining golden colour as it fell. The colour reflected on the sea.

'I don't think she will. I think our Lisa has inner strength.'

'I hope you're right.'

Gina looked up at him and her mouth tightened. He sounded almost accusing. . .

'It's the best I can do,' she said simply. 'If you can think of some other way. . .'

He sighed and dug his hands deep into his trouser pockets. 'I can't, of course,' he admitted. He looked at her and managed a smile. 'Thank God we have a paediatrician in our midst.'

'What I'm doing has little to do with me being a paediatrician.'

'I know.' He frowned. 'How to cope with grief. . . So, how did you learn that, Dr Buchanan?'

'The hard way.'

'The way Lisa's learning it?'

'Yes. Though. . . Though I was older.'

'How old?'

'Eight.'

He whistled soundlessly. 'Your mother?'

Gina's face closed. 'Yes.'

'But you still had your father?'

'No.' She shrugged. 'My father left for good when I was four. He was in the Navy and we cramped his style. When my mother was diagnosed with cancer they let him know—but he didn't come. I haven't seen him since I was four.'

'So you were left with no one?'

'Not quite. I had Wayne's mother. . .and Wayne.'

'Well, well. . .' His dark eyes softened with understanding. 'I begin to see.'

'No.' Gina shook her head. 'You don't. Or you wouldn't be flippant about marriage and commitment.'

'Gina, I'm not the least bit flippant.'

'Ha!' She backed away from those searching eyes, the face that saw too darned much for her liking. Then the door swung open behind her, giving her an excuse to turn.

Lisa was standing on the doorstep, one hand clutching her tiger, the other holding the photograph that Gina had placed on the pillow beside her. 'I'm ready to go h——'

She stopped. Her tear-stained face crumpled again and Struan was with her in one lithe movement. He lifted her high and swung her, and then popped her down on her feet again.

'You're ready to come down to the beach to have a picnic tea,' he told her firmly. He motioned to the tiger. 'With Sam, if Sam promises not to eat too much.'

The tears stopped. Lisa looked doubtfully at Struan. 'Silly,' she said uncertainly. 'Sam doesn't eat.'

'He's decidedly silly,' Gina agreed with her. 'I've been telling Dr Maitland he's very, very silly for as long as I've known him. A great hairy twit. . .'

'Here!'

'He's not hairy!'

The two voices spoke in unison and Gina looked from one to the other and laughed. It was a laugh of happiness. Lisa could go forward from this moment.

To where. . .?

To her aunt, Gina told herself firmly, and then suddenly realised where her thoughts were taking her.

For Lisa, an aunt who didn't want her.

For Gina, Wayne. . .

'Come on, then, Dr Maitland,' she told Struan, and her voice was suddenly tight with pain. 'Let's get this picnic over with.'

'Hey, Dr Buchanan. . .' Struan looked down at her in concern and his eyebrows furrowed. 'I sense an attitude problem. A picnic's supposed to be fun.'

Gina bit her lip and nodded, managing a smile. 'Fun,' she agreed.

Maybe. . .

CHAPTER FIVE

THE beach was lovely. Struan drove the car down to a sheltered cove a few hundred yards from the house. Here the grass sloped gently down to sand, making it easy for Gina to manoeuvre herself almost to the place Struan had decreed as 'the place for a picnic'.

'It's very important to choose the right spot,' he told Lisa, swooping the little girl up and lifting her across the sand. After over a week of bed-rest, the child's legs weren't strong enough to cope with sand. She clutched Sam Tiger, though. Sam was staying in Lisa's arms for now and forever. 'We don't want hordes of hungry ants, or armies of giant sand-hoppers, or herds of scavenging gulls. . .'

'It's flocks,' Lisa giggled. 'You have flocks of sea-gulls. It's herds of elephants.'

'Might well be the same thing if the gulls are hungry enough.' Struan smiled down at her. 'You can't be too careful. And, even though we have Sam Tiger, I think we'd better keep our heads low.'

'Dr Buchanan's stuck. . .' Lisa looked back and saw Gina's crutches sink into soft sand.

'I know. She's my second passenger.' Struan placed Lisa with care on to the rug and came back for Gina.

'I'm all right,' Gina said breathlessly. 'I can manage.'

'Liar.'

Without further ado, like Lisa, she was swept up into strong arms.

It was a weird sensation. The sensation of being cherished. . . Gina subsided helplessly against Struan's strong chest and tried to block out the unwelcome sensations the nearness of Struan's body produced in hers.

He took longer than he had taken with Lisa. Struan strode slowly to the rug, but then stood looking down at the girl in his arms. Her long blonde hair whipped around her face in the light breeze blowing in from the sea. It blew back momentarily, leaving the dressing above her eye bare.

'Murderous cretin,' Struan said suddenly, his eyes darkening.

'Who, me?'

'Don't be a fool.' His face dropped suddenly and his lips touched the dressing. 'I should have hit him harder.'

'I wish you had. . .' The memory of Lloyd flashed before Gina and her eyes dulled.

'Damn. . .' Struan swore softly. 'I shouldn't. . .' He placed her tenderly down. 'Me and my big mouth,' he muttered. He looked across at Lisa. 'Tell you what, Lisa. Let's make a rule. For tonight there's not to be one single sad thought. Nothing. Let's Sam and you and Dr Buchanan and me have ourselves a feast, and leave the rest of the world out of it. Good idea?'

Lisa considered. She looked from Gina to Struan and back again. Finally she looked consideringly at Sam.

'I might have already had my tea,' she said slowly, as though confessing something she didn't want to admit. 'At the hospital.'

'But that's part of the outside world,' Struan told her. 'That's part of what we have to forget. Deal, Lisa?'

'You mean it doesn't matter?'

'Nothing matters.' Struan's voice was suddenly intense. He took Lisa's hands in his, glanced at Gina and then back to Lisa. 'Nothing except now. OK?'

'OK,' said Lisa.

The hospital kitchen had done them proud.

'Mrs O'Donnell's a friend of mine,' Struan said, and

grinned when Gina's eyes widened at what he had brought. A huge quiche was still warm, wrapped in layers of teatowel. There were crunchy rolls spread thickly with golden butter, and crispy, bite-sized salad with an esoteric mix of the produce of the hospital garden. Tiny lamingtons filled with cream, which would tempt the most jaded appetite, and a huge bottle of lemonade which appeared from a separate cooler.

'That's your tipple, little one,' Struan told Lisa. 'I've something else planned for Dr Buchanan.' And a bottle of ice-cold wine appeared, complete with two wine-glasses.

'This isn't a picnic,' Gina said accusingly. 'It's a party.'

'So I should think.' Struan filled wine-glasses and lemonade beaker and raised his glass to Lisa and Gina. 'Tonight deserves a party. Here's to the rest of our lives. Starting now. The future. . .'

It was a shrewd, intuitive toast. Lisa looked uncertainly from Struan to Gina, and then looked down at her Sam Tiger. Struan's glass was still raised, waiting.

'The future,' he said again, and sent a message to Gina with his eyes.

Gina took a deep breath. The future. . . Stability. Permanence. Wayne. 'The future,' she said, and she couldn't quite keep the tremor from her voice.

Lisa picked Sam Tiger up with her free hand. She knew what she was expected to say, but it took sheer courage to say it. Her bottom lip wobbled, but she said it all the same.

'The future. . . .'

And then the tremors were forgotten as they tucked into their feast.

It was a magic night. They ate their fill and then made the king of all sandcastles. It was vast, with moats and turrets and seaweed gardens. Struan filled the big cooler with sea-water, trudging up the beach over and over again as he filled the moat, and then groaning with dismay as his water seeped down into the soft sand.

'You're not allowed to stop,' Lisa ordered. 'The dragons will reach the castle if you stop now. . .'

Struan sighed theatrically, grinning down at the two girls. 'I've always fancied myself as the protector of maidens against dragons,' he mused. 'But I didn't think it'd take this form.'

Lisa wasn't impressed. 'Quick,' she squealed. 'Quick. It's nearly dry.'

And Struan set off once again for the shallows while Gina dissolved in a delicious bubble of laughter.

Struan had rolled his trousers up but he never quite managed to make the trip without getting wet. He strode up and down the beach, and Gina felt herself almost physically ache to walk down into the water with him.

It's the lack of the beard, she told herself crossly.

He made you feel like this before the beard came off. It's chemistry. . .answered another inner voice.

Pure animal something. . . Get a hold on yourself, Dr Buchanan!

And then, finally, the tide took over, seeping into their moat entry and freeing Struan from his labours. He sank down on to the sand in gratitude and watched while Gina held Lisa on her lap and told the child a story.

Dragons and princes. Fairies and long-ago battles, handsome knights and gallant steeds with flying manes, and the splendour of flags and glinting armour. Gina dredged up stories that she'd heard long ago from her mother and had forgotten she even knew.

Lisa listened, wide-eyed, cradled against Gina and clutching her beloved Sam Tiger. And finally the eyelids drooped, lower and lower, and she drifted into sleep.

Gina's voice faded. She looked down at the sleeping

child and her heart twisted within her to the point where she thought she was going to weep.

'Don't stop,' Struan said gently. 'I want to know what happened to Prince Lochnivar and his beautiful Ethel.'

'They got married and had babies and he washed nappies while Ethel joined the PTA,' Gina managed, winking away a tear.

'You're kidding?'

'Would I kid about something so important?' Gina looked down at Lisa and her voice faltered. 'Struan, what will. . .? What is. . .?'

'What is going to happen to Lisa?' Struan sighed. He was sprawled on the rug beside Gina and his hand came over to touch the child's sleeping face. 'I don't know,' he admitted. 'You've done well so far, Dr Buchanan.'

'It occurs to me, though. . .' Gina bit her lip. 'I've taken away her defences. While she wasn't walking or speaking we could keep her in hospital. Now. . .'

'We can keep her in hospital a good while longer. The only one who'll object will be your Wayne.'

'Wayne won't object.'

'Want to bet? It mucks up his precious funding through case mix. He loathes long-term patients. And if he figures she's well enough to be shipped off to foster-care. . .'

'There are excellent foster-care families.'

'There are,' Struan agreed. 'But none in this town. None where Lisa can keep any sort of relationship she already has—or any links with her mother's memory.'

'But her aunt. . .'

'Sandra.' Struan nodded. 'That's why I want more time. If I can persuade Sandra and her husband to take her. . . At least then Lisa will feel she still has those links.'

'But they don't want her.'

'Maybe now she's recovering they will,' Struan said bleakly, and by his tone Gina knew he didn't believe it.

'Struan. . .'

His eyes lifted to hers. The sun had sunk to a distant glow of remembrance on the horizon. The night was still warm but Gina shivered.

'Yes, my love.' His eyes deepened, caressing. . .

'Struan, no. . .' She shook her head in protest. Ignore it, she told herself. It's a line he uses. How many women had he called 'my love'? 'Struan, tell me what happened the day Lisa's mother died. Why was Lisa alone in the house for so long? It doesn't make sense.'

'Why doesn't it make sense?'

'Because Jenny loved her daughter.' Gina looked down at the elfin figure cradled on her lap. 'That she should kill herself with no provision at all. . .' She took a deep breath. 'Struan, when my mother was diagnosed as having terminal cancer, she spent all the time left to her worrying about who would take care of me. I had one nightmare night at the end, because everything happened so fast, but not what Lisa had to endure— nearly two days. It doesn't make sense that Jenny didn't worry as well.'

'She did.'

Gina's eyes flew up to his. 'How? What do you mean?'

'Jenny asked Sandra to have Lisa for the day. Pleaded. . . Told Sandra she had to have a day to herself, but she didn't tell her why. I gather Sandra was annoyed because she'd looked after Lisa less than two weeks before—when Jenny went to Melbourne by herself. Anyway, Jenny dropped Lisa at Sandra's house at nine in the morning and the agreement was that Sandra would bring Lisa home after tea that night. And Sandra said she was odd. . . Said Jenny made her promise that if anything happened to her, Sandra would care for Lisa. So Sandra promised—thinking it would never happen, of course. An idle promise.

'Then, as far as we can tell, Jenny went home and took a massive overdose. She would have been dead by lunch-time. Her theory was that Aunty Sandra would bring the child home and find her. Only Aunty Sandra was in a hurry and she was still cross. Even though the house was in darkness, she dropped Lisa off at the gate and left her there.' Struan shrugged. 'It's a lonely spot—too far for Lisa to walk and get help. Her school-teacher assumed she was ill, so two days later drove up to see what the problem was. If we didn't have a conscientious school-teacher——' He broke off. 'Well, a nasty little story, but it happens.'

'Sandra can't have Lisa.'

'Gina. . .'

'She can't.' Gina put her face down suddenly and buried it in the child's soft curls. 'How dare she. . .?'

Struan moved to a sitting position. He touched Gina lightly on the face. 'Hey, Dr Buchanan. We need a little professional detachment here.'

'I don't have any.'

'Are you like this with all your patients?'

Gina closed her eyes. 'Of course not. It's just. . .'

'Just that Lisa has struck at pain that's too close to yours? You know what's in store for her?'

'Yes. . .'

There was a long, long silence.

'At least,' Gina said finally, 'at least Lisa will know that her mum tried to make provision. . .'

'By committing suicide.' Struan laughed shortly. 'A lot of comfort. It often seems to me that suicide is the ultimate selfishness.'

'So there has to be a reason.' Gina took a deep breath. 'It's important—for Lisa—for the future that we find out what it is.'

'It's none of our business, Dr Buchanan.'

Gina's eyes flashed. 'That's a cop-out, Struan Maitland, and you know it.'

'And you never cop out?'

Gina stared. 'What. . .what do you mean?'

'I mean, isn't that what you're doing marrying our Wayne?' Struan lifted the sleeping Lisa from Gina's lap and laid her gently down on the rug. He looped the other side of the blanket over her, cocooning her in warmth. Then he turned back to Gina. 'It is, you know,' he said conversationally. 'Copping out.'

'Now who's digging into what's none of their business?'

'Oh, but it is.' He reached out and strong hands gripped hers. 'It is my business that the woman I intend to marry has got herself engaged to someone else.'

'Don't. . .' She pulled her hands back but she was held in a grip of iron. 'Don't be ridiculous.'

'It's not me who's ridiculous, my lovely Gina. It's Wayne. A more ridiculous, pompous little man I've never elsewhere encountered—and you say you'll marry him.'

'Wayne. . .' Gina took a deep breath. 'Wayne is more dependable than any person I've ever met. If you only knew. . .'

'So tell me.' His hands still gripped.

Gina tugged futilely back. 'Let me go.'

'Not until you tell me why Wayne's so dependable.'

'He keeps his promises. . .' Gina was close to tears. 'For heaven's sake. . .'

'What promises?' Polite interest, but the hands didn't move. If anything, the grip tightened.

Gina closed her eyes. 'All his promises,' she said bleakly. Then, as the silence stretched out between them, she made herself go on.

'He's the only one who ever did,' she managed. 'My father. . . Well, he was the most exciting man. I could see why my mother loved him. He promised. . .he promised to take care of us always. Well, that only lasted until he met another woman. And then my mother promised that she'd be there always, and she got cancer. . . Unfair of me to hold that against her— but as I child I did. And then. . . Well, my mother's best friend was Wayne's mother. Shirley promised my mother she'd take care of me, and that only lasted until the funeral. Then I was shipped off to foster-homes. But Wayne. . . Wayne promised he'd visit me once a month forever—and he did. Wherever I was— and I ended up in some pretty weird places—Wayne would come.' She bit her lip. 'You can't imagine how much that meant to me.'

'So you're marrying him out of gratitude?'

'No!' She pulled her hands back, and this time he released her. 'I'm marrying Wayne because he's kind and caring and compassionate—and he'll never let me down. If I have children he'll be responsible and. . . and. . .'

Her voice trailed away. She felt behind her for her crutches and struggled to her feet. 'Please. . . Please, Dr Maitland, I want to go home.'

'There's more to marriage than dependability.'

'Oh, yes. You'd say that, wouldn't you? You and your damned bike and your beard. . .'

'I haven't got a beard.' He sounded aggrieved. 'I thought you'd noticed.'

'Well, you're still———'

'Dangerous?'

'Yes. If you must know, yes. You're just the sort of man I made up my mind I'd never marry.'

'Because you'd be hurt all over again if anything happened—if I walked out on you?'

'No. . .'

'You're not game to take another chance, are you, Dr Buchanan?' Struan had risen to his feet, and his arms came out to steady her as she wobbled on her crutches on the soft sand. 'You gave your heart to your father and had it broken—and then your mother left you. So you figure you'll go through life in splendid isolation.'

'That's not true. Wayne and I will have children. . .'

'But you'll look after them. Who'll look after you?'

'Wayne. And I'll care for him.'

'Wayne. . .' Struan shook his head. 'Gina Buchanan, Wayne is as capable of cherishing as a cold fish. He'll spend his life worrying about budgets and neck-ties and what people are thinking of him. If you step one inch out of line he'll walk away from you as soon as look at you. Sure, he's been good to you. He promised, and Wayne sees a promise as a sacred cow. Honesty? Try fiddling the books to give an elderly lady a night in hospital because her husband's dying and she can't bear to go home—then see what sort of honesty Wayne has.'

Gina let her crutches drop. They were useless in the sand and Struan's hands were on her sides, holding her up. She clapped her hands over her ears.

'I don't want to listen,' she said desperately. 'I don't. . .'

'You don't want to know what Wayne's all about? Good grief, woman, you're going to marry the man. It's about time you found out.'

'I know all I need to know.'

He shook his head and his dark eyes gleamed with sudden mischief. 'I bet you don't, Dr Buchanan. I bet you don't even know what he's like in bed. Do you?' And then, at the look on her face, he gave a crack of laughter. 'I knew it. Our Wayne wouldn't so sully himself. I bet he doesn't even know what a condom is. When you're married he'll send you off to get a supply of the Pill, because he can't bear thinking of such unpleasant things. And twice a week, at the most, with the lights safely off, he'll have sex in the missionary position——'

'I don't have to listen to this!' Gina's face was flushed to brilliant red. She lifted her good foot and kicked for all she was worth. Her sandal hit his leg, but without the force she'd intended. Her other leg gave, and without Struan's hands she would have fallen.

'Temper, temper, Dr Buchanan.'

'Take me home.'

'You're beautiful when you're angry.'

'I said——'

'Do you really know what you're missing?'

He stared down at her for a long, long moment, and then, before Gina realised what he intended, he bent his head and kissed her.

This was not the way Wayne kissed.

This was not the way Gina had ever been kissed in her life before. Lie back and think of England? No way, with this mouth on hers, these hands holding her body to his in urgent possession and this strong, male body moulding to hers.

She was rigid with shock. Gina's hands dropped to her sides. She should fight. . . But how could she fight him with a gammy leg and when he was so damned big?

And when she didn't want to fight one bit.

Dear God, what was she doing? What was she thinking?

It didn't make any difference. Gina's body was responding all on its own to the man—the night—the warm sea air and the sound of the surf behind them.

He tasted like the sea. . .

The fleeting, perilous thought flashed across her mind and she was lost in a vortex of emotions she had no way of describing. She had never felt like this. Never! She felt her body shudder, and she knew that it wasn't fear. It was pure, absolute desire.

The kiss deepened. It stretched on and on, a kiss

with no beginning and no end. Please, God. . . Please God, no end. Gina's hands came up to hold his face to hers. Her fingers felt the new-shaved smoothness of his skin. He'd done this for her? Some tiny, triumphant part of self screamed it home to her and she gloried in the knowledge. Just for this moment. . .

He wanted her. Just for this moment she could accept that she was wanted. The sea beat out its gentle rhythm and it seemed to keep in rhythm with her heart. This was how it could be. . .

This was how it had been for her mother. . .

The thought was enough. Gina froze in Struan's grip and he drew back.

'What is it, my love?' he asked softly, and his eyes were so damned caring that it made Gina's heart turn over. She turned away fast, averting her gaze from that look.

'Please. . . Please. . .'

'Don't upset your carefully laid plans? Is that what you're asking, my Gina?'

'No. Yes! Just. . .just leave me alone, Struan Maitland. I don't want you anywhere near me. I want. . .'

'You want Wayne?'

'Yes!'

Struan shook his head. 'You don't want him. You just haven't the courage to tell him so.'

'That's not true. If I didn't want to marry him I wouldn't.'

'Gina, you're under the biggest obligation of your life to that man. So big it's threatening to break you. And he's engineered it all himself.'

'He hasn't engineered anything. He was kind. . .' Gina drew in her breath. 'The only one. . .'

'Maybe in the past. But not now.'

'Are you telling me you're kind?' Gina demanded. 'That's ridiculous. You're nothing but a bully, Struan

Maitland, sweeping all before you when they're unfortunate enough to get in your road.' She knelt down on the sand and started gathering the remnants of the picnic together. 'Now, take me home. I've had enough attempts at romantic seduction for one day. From here on. . . From here on I only want to see you when you need to consult about a patient. And that's all, Struan Maitland.'

He stood watching her, his dark eyes fathomless. Finally the corners of his wide mouth twisted up in a rueful smile. 'Well, that's going to be a bit difficult, Dr Buchanan. What about the weekend?'

'What about the weekend?' she said blankly.

'We're going to Melbourne.'

'We——'

'You and me, Dr Buchanan. I'm going down to see Lloyd again, and I assumed you'd wish to see him personally as well. So I've booked two seats on Friday night's flight. Accommodation in Melbourne and back on Sunday.'

'But. . .' Gina gazed up at him in stupefaction. 'But I don't want to go to Melbourne.'

'You've agreed to start work for us on Monday.' Struan's voice suddenly became harsh. 'Don't you feel like making the effort to see Lloyd before that?' He frowned. 'If you're not grateful to the boy you damned well ought to be.'

'But. . .'

'But what, Dr Buchanan?'

There was nothing to say. Nothing to counter his carefully laid plans. Lloyd was facing paraplegia because of her, and she had to go. She must.

'Fine,' she said tightly.

'Fine,' Struan repeated. 'No, "Thank you for organising this, Dr Maitland"? No, "What a good idea"?'

'No.'

He shrugged and then his face broke into a grin. He knelt beside Gina and started to help her pack. 'Cheer up, Dr Buchanan,' he told her, and his smile told her he knew just what she was thinking. 'I know you'll find visiting Lloyd an ordeal, but there's always my company to cheer you up.'

Gina picked up the big plastic cooler. It was heavy—still half-full of sea-water.

The temptation was too great to resist. She aimed it and threw the cold water straight at Struan Maitland's laughing face.

CHAPTER SIX

AT LEAST she was off her crutches.

That was all the comfort Gina could find as she waited for the plane on Friday night. Lesley had removed her stitches, bemused by Gina's point-blank refusal to let Struan Maitland anywhere near his handiwork.

'He's done a lovely job,' Lesley had assured her. 'When the swelling's subsided you'll be left with a hairline scar. Considering the tear that dreadful man inflicted, it's a beautiful repair.' She had smiled coaxingly up at Gina. 'Why not let Struan see his end result?'

'Because his end result is on my thigh,' Gina had said crossly. She'd met Lesley's bemused look. 'And I can't divorce Struan Maitland, doctor, from Struan Maitland, arrogant toad.'

'Oh, dear.' Lesley's kindly face wrinkled into a smile of understanding. 'Like that, is it?'

'It's not like anything of the sort,' Gina retorted, and Lesley's smile deepened.

'No, dear. Whatever you say.'

Gina regarded her suspiciously. 'You mean, the customer's always right?'

'Something like that. Only I'm not asking for payment.' Lesley looked down at the wound with satisfaction. 'Not when you're our newest associate.' She rose and smiled down at Gina. 'Enjoy your trip to Melbourne. Give all our love to Lloyd, won't you, dear, and come back to us ready for work?'

Gina nodded. The other doctors in the town had been run ragged since Lloyd had been injured.

'Struan really shouldn't be going away again, leaving you with all the work.'

Lesley shook her head. 'Struan's worked every night this week. The man's exhausted. If he doesn't have some time off, he'll drop.'

Exhausted. . . It was a new way of looking at Struan Maitland, and when he strode across the tarmac, with moments to spare before the plane took off, Gina noticed the shadowing of his face for the first time. He did look tired.

'You're late,' Wayne told Struan accusingly. He'd reluctantly agreed with Gina that she had an obligation to see Lloyd, but that didn't make him happy about the company she was keeping on the way. He had driven her to the airport three quarters of an hour before the plane was due to leave and had been filling the waiting-time with a stirring description of his last three chess victories. Gina was almost grateful to see Struan. Almost. . .

'Haven't missed a plane yet,' Struan told Wayne, with cheerful good humour. He ran his eyes approvingly over Gina's slim body, his look warming at her wide white skirt and broderie anglaise blouse. 'Very nice,' he said softly.

Gina flushed. It still hurt to wear jeans, but that was what she should have had on now. Or a suit of armour. Or. . . Or a chastity belt, her evil mind whispered, and she caught herself on a gasp.

'Let's. . . Let's go.'

'I couldn't agree more.' Struan tossed his bag into the cargo hold, greeted the pilot with the familiarity of long acquaintance, and then turned back to grip Wayne's hand.

'Don't worry, mate. I'll take care of her for you.'

I'll bet, Gina thought grimly.

* * *

Gina had schooled herself to be rigidly polite for the duration of the flight. Her plans were foiled, however, by Struan. He strapped himself in, yawned once, and slept. He didn't open his eyes until they touched down in Melbourne.

'Good flight?' he enquired of Gina, and she scowled at him.

'It would have been if you didn't snore.'

'I don't snore.' His deep, dark eyes widened in protesting innocence. 'I never snore.' Then, to Gina's horror, he stopped the stewardess mid-aisle. 'Excuse me, miss. I've been accused of snoring. Can I have an independent arbitrator, please?'

Gina flushed to the roots of her hair. Honestly, the man was impossible. And so damned attractive. . . The stewardess looked down at Struan's good-looking face and broke into her very nicest smile.

'Of course you didn't, sir.' She flashed a glance at Gina, which showed clearly that she couldn't understand Gina's luck in having such a hunk beside her, and asked what on earth the man was thinking of, choosing such a drab little companion. With a bandage on her face, for heaven's sake. . . She looked down at the passenger-list in her hand and her smile became understanding. Dr Struan Maitland. 'You're just bringing a patient down to Melbourne, are you, sir?' she asked.

Gina winced, but Struan's smile widened. 'I am,' he grinned. He lowered his voice to a stage whisper. 'Poor girl suffers from delusions. Seems to think I snore. . .'

The hostess laughed with him and moved reluctantly on.

'How. . .how dare you?'

'There's no bucket of water handy, either,' Struan said blandly. He rose into the aisle. The last of the passengers were leaving the plane but Struan was in no hurry. He put his hand on Gina's arm. 'Now, shall you come quietly, or shall I ask the hostess to fetch a strait-jacket?'

By the time they emerged from the airport it was too late to visit Lloyd.

'Hotel, sleep, breakfast and Lloyd, in that order,' Struan said as he hailed a cab.

'You've decided that?' Gina was still vacillating between laughter and indignation.

'Would you like to change the order?'

'No.' She slid into the back seat of the taxi, sliding as far across from Struan's abominable presence as she could. 'Where. . .where are we staying?'

'Baron's Hall.'

'Baron's Hall!' Gina's voice rose on a squeak. 'Have you any idea how much they charge?'

'I'm paying. Don't worry, Dr Buchanan. Your beloved Wayne need never see his hard-earned money going on frivolous living.'

'Wayne. . . Wayne wouldn't be paying. It'd be my money.'

'It's still Wayne's hard-earned money,' Struan said blandly. 'He's worked hard for your income.'

'He——' Gina's fists clenched, and Struan's eyes gleamed across at her.

'Go on. Hit me, Dr Buchanan. You'd love to, wouldn't you?'

'Yes,' she said bitterly. 'But only if I had the ability to hurt you. Badly.'

Struan's smile faded. He looked across at her in the dim light cast in the taxi's interior by the lights of the city.

'Oh, you have that all right,' he said softly. 'But I don't think you know how very much.'

Visiting hours at Melbourne Central's spinal unit were from ten-thirty, and it was only moments after that when Gina and Struan arrived.

Struan looked rested and relaxed, in casual trousers and a short-sleeved checked shirt that made him seem broader across the chest than he already was. Rested and relaxed wouldn't describe Gina, though. She had shadows that no amount of make-up would hide. She'd spent the night worrying about Lloyd and achingly aware of the adjoining room—with a door linking her to Struan. She'd locked it and stuck a chair under it, but still it seemed threatening. . .

If her body had been allowed to hold sway she would have unlocked the thing, Her body. . .

She had writhed in her bed and tried to think of Wayne, but nothing came. Lloyd. . . Struan. . . Concern for Lloyd. But what was she feeling for Struan?

She'd breakfasted in her room, determined to show Struan Maitland that she wanted none of his company. To her annoyance, he had seemed not to notice. Whatever he had done he hadn't contacted her, and a few moments before ten the hotel receptionist had called.

'Dr Maitland's waiting in Reception,' she'd said sweetly. 'Could you come down, please?'

Fine, Gina had thought, savagely applying her mascara with such a ferocious thrust that she'd run a line of black down her face. All I need to do is salute. . .

Her anger was partly fed by nerves, she acknowledged as she and Struan walked through the long hospital corridors towards Lloyd's ward. How would she cope with this? What did you say to a boy who'd almost died for you?

In the end it was easy.

Lloyd was in a vast eight-bed ward. Each of the patients was, like Lloyd, flat on their back and rigidly immobilised with traction. The ward resembled nothing so much as a huge gym—or torture chamber, Gina thought grimly. The rack had nothing on some of these pieces of equipment.

He was darker than Gina remembered him. He had

the same boy's face she would see in front of her all her life, but a man's body, and a man's suffering behind the bright, eager eyes.

'Well, well. . .' He spoke first, his eyes lighting at the sight of Struan. 'Another weekend absconding from work, Dr Maitland. . .' And then he saw Gina beside him and his smile slipped. He took a deep breath, wet his lips with his tongue, and the smile crept back.

'My damsel in distress,' he whispered. 'They've been telling me it wasn't worth it—risking my damned neck—but now. . .' His pain-filled eyes creased in welcome and his hand lifted weakly to take hers. 'Hey, bring on more dragons. I'll take them on in force.'

'Enough, you young fire-eater,' Struan growled, but by the look on his face Gina could tell Struan was almost as affected by Lloyd's bravery as she was. 'I'm on dragon-duty for a while.'

'Yeah. . . Now we've got the biggest, nastiest dragon locked up, in comes Struan Maitland, waving sword. . .' He smiled. 'What a hero,' he told Gina.

'It's you who's the hero,' Gina said softly. She gripped his hand and bent to kiss him, her eyes filling with tears. 'Of all the mad, brave, wonderful things to do. . .'

'Hey.' His hand tightened. 'You're not supposed to cry, lady. Struan tells me you're a doctor. I haven't had a doctor near me who hasn't been saying things like "Chin up" and "There's lots worse off than you, young Lloyd" and "We'll soon have you right as a trivet. . ."' His voice faltered and faded to nothing. 'Soon. . .' he whispered, and there was fear in his voice.

'So tell me.' Gina fought to hold back tears and found professionalism. Just. 'Tell me the prognosis.' She sank on to the visitor's chair but her hand didn't leave his.

He looked down at her, and the fear faded a little. 'You really are a doctor, then?'

'Paediatrician,' Struan growled. 'Not a real doctor. I always reckon they're something more akin to a vet.' He was lifting the chart from the end of the bed.

'Heh,' Lloyd expostulated. 'You're not supposed to read that. All my intimate details.'

'I won't tell the lady when you last opened your bowels,' Struan grinned. 'At least, I won't if you tell us what the orthopods are saying.'

Lloyd hesitated. Fear trickled back. 'It's still. . .still too soon to say. . .'

'If it was rotten news you'd know it by now. You have feeling?'

'In my left leg. Some. . .patches in my right. I can feel but can't make the damned things move.'

'You'd be a damned fool to try at the moment.'

'Oh, yeah. . .' Lloyd grimaced at the traction holding him rigidly in position. 'But I should be able to wiggle my toes. Should.'

'Not with swelling round the break. And it can take months to subside. You've fractured your spine, Lloyd. It's going to take a long time for the swelling to reduce completely.'

'I know that.' Lloyd was silent for a long time. Neither Gina nor Struan spoke. It was as if he was making up his mind.

'I've been lying here wondering if I can practise medicine from a wheelchair,' he said finally. He sighed and met Struan's look. 'No. The orthopods haven't said it's hopeless. They say there's a good chance of eventual recovery. But there's still a chance I might not walk again.' He grimaced. 'You know, two weeks ago I thought I was immortal.'

'Bloody young fool. . .'

'Yeah, well, you'd know, wouldn't you, Struan? You

have a whole ten years on me and you sound a hundred.'

'I broke my leg at twenty,' Struan said grimly. 'And discovered the bitter truth—that the body's only as good as the head in control—and sometimes not even that good.'

Gina couldn't resist. 'So how did you break your leg?'

'Paragliding.'

'Oh, yeah. . . Very sensible!' Lloyd grinned. 'There's a guy in the next bed who did that. Only he broke his back instead of his leg.' He looked at Gina. 'At least my reason's sensible—gorgeous, in fact. . .' He raised his hand and lifted her hair from the scar above her eye. 'Though I didn't stop him.'

'You did,' Gina said solidly. 'He thought he'd killed you. They all took off in fright—and then our Dr Maitland came along and polished off the pieces.' She smiled down at him. 'Lloyd, I can't ever begin to thank you. . .'

'Just being here is enough,' he told her. 'Plus. . . Struan tells me you're holding my job.'

'As of Monday,' she promised. 'For as long as it takes.'

'Yeah. . .' The closed look came down over pain-filled eyes. 'As long as it takes. It could be for bloody ever.'

'The Gundowring Hospital corridors are big enough for a wheelchair, if it comes to that,' Struan told him.

'I can't practise medicine in a wheelchair.'

'Why not?'

'Because. . .' Lloyd turned away, his face bleak. 'God, Struan, it doesn't bear thinking of. It doesn't.'

'So don't.' Struan's hand came down and gripped the young man's shoulder—hard. 'Concentrate on the toes. One thing at a time, young Lloyd.' He looked up as the ward door swung open and two nurses

appeared with a trolley of steaming water. 'Now, if
I'm not mistaken this is your bath. We won't keep you
from two nubile young wenches wishing to pander to
your bodily whims, young Lloyd.'

'You're staying the weekend?'

'Yes,' Struan promised. 'And we'll be back this
evening, won't we, Dr Buchanan?'

Gina nodded her agreement, and Lloyd looked from
one to the other with interest.

'I saved her,' he said cautiously. 'This doesn't seem
right. That you get the damsel in distress. . .'

'You saved her for me.' Struan grinned. 'Some day
I'll give you half my kingdom.' And he ushered the
dumbstruck Gina out of the door.

He took her straight to the cafeteria and ordered
strong, hot coffee. Gina took it gratefully—passively.
Her hands weren't quite steady, she noticed, as she
held the steaming mug.

'He may well be fine,' Struan told her gently. He
knew instinctively where her thoughts were going.
'It's just time. . . I've known spinal bruising—and
recovery—to take up to two years.'

Two years. . . Gina looked up at Struan and then
bleakly back to her coffee-cup. Two years out of a
young man's life. . .

'They're not wasted, you know,' Struan continued.
'Not wasted years. If he gets up on his feet after this
he'll be one of the best physicians in the country. First-
hand experience of pain is the best teacher.'

'Oh, great,' Gina whispered. 'You mean, he should
be thankful. . .?'

'No. But maybe he will be.'

Silence. Gina finished her coffee and stared at the
dregs. Finally she pushed the mug aside.

'I've things to do,' she told him. 'While I'm in
Melbourne. Shall I meet you back here?'

Surprisingly he agreed. 'Sure. Six p.m. back here,

and we'll go to dinner afterwards.'

She was too surprised by his agreement to her proposal to demur at his. Dinner was a long way away.

'Fine.' She dragged herself to her feet. Without her crutches her hip was starting to ache. She'd go back to the hotel for a rest—but first there were things to do. 'I'll see you then.'

The doctor's card had been lying in Gina's bag since the day she went to Lisa's house. She had rung once but had been given a very brusque, 'The doctor doesn't discuss patients over the phone, and we have no one of that name on our files anyway.' Now. . .

The address was only a mile from the city centre. Gina took a taxi, sitting gratefully back on the soft upholstery and letting her aching thigh rest.

A wide, tree-lined street. . . An unobtrusive sign set into a brick fence before a solid, weatherboard house. 'Dr Elizabeth Chong MB BS FRACGP'.

The same as the card in Jenny's drawer.

There was a small surgery attached to the side of the house. Dr Chong, it seemed, worked from home. On Saturday morning it was locked and looked deserted. Gina looked down at the card in her hand again. This was a gamble, and she hoped to heaven she was right. She swung the side gate open and went through.

'Are you here to see Mummy? She's not working today.' A young boy of about four wheeled up to her on his tricycle and regarded her with interest. 'What have you done to your face?'

'I cut it.' Gina smiled down at him. 'Three stitches.'

'Wow! I watched Mum do stitches once. Yuk!'

A young woman was coming from the house, wiping her hands on a teatowel as she came. She stopped dead when she saw Gina. 'It's a ghost,' she said faintly.

'Liz!' Gina's face broke into a delighted grin of

recognition. Liz Cholmondley. She hadn't seen her since university. . . She stared down at the card. 'It says here, Elizabeth Chong,' she said accusingly.

'Wouldn't you rather be Chong than Cholmondley?' Liz retorted, coming forward to give her old friend a swift hug. 'I know it's unusual for doctors to take their husband's surnames, but it's a darned sight easier.' And then she grinned. 'And in a migrant area of Melbourne it has all sorts of financial benefits. My patients get an awful shock when they meet white-skinned, red-headed Elizabeth Chong for the first time, having chosen her name from the phone book—but once I have them in my clutches I hardly ever lose them.'

'I'll bet.' Gina sighed happily. This would make things so much easier.

'So come in and have some coffee,' Liz ordered, tucking her hand through her arm. 'To what do I owe the pleasure? And what on earth have you been doing to yourself?'

Ten minutes later she was shaking her head. 'Gina, I don't think. . . It's lovely to see you, but I think you're on a wild-goose chase. I've never treated a Jenny Gibson.' She frowned. 'Just a moment and I'll check. . .' She went through to her surgery and was back two minutes later. 'No one of that name.'

Gina nodded. 'She might not have been using her real name, Liz.' She lifted the photograph from her bag. 'Do you recognise her?'

There was a long, long silence. Liz stared at the photograph for so long that Gina almost thought she had forgotten Gina's presence. Finally Liz laid the photograph back on the table and her eyes were haunted.

'She suicided?'

'Yes.'

'When?'

'Nearly two weeks ago.'

Liz moistened her lips. She picked up her coffee-mug and the coffee slopped over the side. When Gina looked up at her friend's face, Liz's eyes were wet with tears.

'Damn. Damn. Damn!'

'You do know her, then?'

'Of course I know her.'

'You saw her more than once?'

Liz nodded. 'I saw her once about six weeks ago. She had her little girl with her—the child who's with her in the picture. She was worried about bleeding. I thought. . .I thought she was using a false name because of the way the child looked at her when I addressed her. Louise Brown, she was calling herself. Also, she didn't have a Medicare card. She said she'd left it at home and she'd pay cash.'

'So. . .'

'So I gave her a pap smear, and then, because I was concerned she mightn't show for subsequent investigation, I organised for a complete scan at the hospital that morning.' Liz sighed. 'She'd been losing weight. She looked. . .I don't know, Gina. . . Sometimes you just get that sinking feeling in the pit of your stomach.'

'And. . .'

Liz shrugged. 'She wouldn't give me a telephone number. She said she'd come in the following week for the results. When the test results came through I drove to the Melbourne address she'd given but it was false. So I had to sit on those damned results and hope she'd come back, and half of me—the cowardly half—didn't want her to show.'

'But she did?'

'Yes. Two weeks later. Without the child this time. I'd cancelled my appointments after hers. I thought. . .I thought I might take her to oncology myself—just to make sure she went—but she simply accepted the results of the tests and then said she didn't want anything else.'

'And the tests. . .?'

'Maybe you've already guessed,' Liz told her. 'Cervical cancer and secondaries in the liver.'

Silence. Liver secondaries. . .

'But. . .but they weren't spotted at post mortem.'

'Was there a post mortem? I don't suppose there would be.' Liz laughed mirthlessly. 'They were looking for death by overdose. Once they'd confirmed that they were hardly likely to go looking for more.'

'I suppose not.' Gina looked over at Elizabeth's bleak face and her hand came out to cover hers. 'Liz, you can't blame yourself for this one.'

'I should have insisted she tell me who she was. . .I should have——'

'People have the right of privacy. She did it her way.'

'So. . .' Liz looked up. 'So you'll keep this to yourself?'

'No.' Gina shook her head. 'Jenny's little girl thinks her mum deserted her through choice, and her sister thinks it was Jenny's decision to dump Lisa on to her. Now. . . It might not make a difference to how Sandra feels—but long-term it will comfort Lisa to know her mother didn't abandon her.'

'I don't think. . .I don't think she had any more than a month or so,' Liz whispered. 'And she would have been ill.'

'And Lisa would have remembered her as ill, instead of bouncy and vivacious and caring. So maybe. . .' Gina shook her head. 'Who knows what's best?' She rose. 'I have to go. Thanks, Liz. You've made the path ahead much easier for Lisa.'

'I'm glad I've done something,' Liz said bitterly. She shoved her hands in her jeans pockets. 'Why the hell did she choose me?'

'Maybe I can guess.' Gina looked out at Liz's

small boy, building sandcastles in his sandpit. Sandcastles. . . 'Maybe it was the name. She was frightened and she guessed what was wrong. She probably decided her course of action before she even came to you the first time. All she wanted from you was confirmation. So she wanted someone who was completely divorced from her life in Gundowring. A Chinese or Malaysian doctor in Melbourne would seem that.'

'Oh, great,' Liz groaned. 'I'm going back to Cholmondley.'

There was nothing more she could do.

Gina returned to the hotel and slept for most of the afternoon, the day's events drifting through her sleep like painful shadows. Finally the clock radio signalled five. She showered and changed—into loose silk trousers in deep black, with a crimson short-sleeved blouse to go with them. It was a little formal for hospital visiting, but Lloyd would enjoy it, she knew, and. . .

And so would Struan. . .

'Stop it, Gina Buchanan. You're a happily engaged woman,' she told her reflection in the mirror.

Not happily, her reflection seemed to say.

'Securely engaged, then. Sensibly engaged. So stop thinking about Struan Maitland or you're going to get yourself into heaps of trouble.'

Heaps of trouble sounds awfully appealing.

'Gina Buchanan!' Gina turned from her reflection with shocked disdain. That anything so attached to her as her own reflection could have such thoughts was enough to shock the socks off her.

It was only her reflection, though. She, Gina Buchanan, could never have such thoughts. Not in a million years!

Could she?

CHAPTER SEVEN

LLOYD was sleeping when Gina arrived back at the hospital and Struan was nowhere to be seen. Gina pulled the chair up beside the bed and settled, content to wait.

He seemed so darned young. . . His fair lashes were long over his closed eyes and his face looked. . . Defenceless, Gina thought sadly. She thought back to the impetuous young man, leaping to her aid only a week ago. Like an overgrown Labrador pup, and now. . . Now he'd been kicked good and solidly. Even if he fully recovered, life would never be the same, Gina knew. His puppyhood had been left behind—and with it his belief in his own invincibility.

And he'd done it for her. . . The thought flashed through Gina's mind that here was someone else who had put her before himself. Previously there had only been Wayne. Wayne, constant every month, regardless. . . Regardless even of chess championships, Wayne had visited, and she knew how much they meant to him.

This boy had put more than chess championships aside. Lloyd had risked everything—and, puppy or not, he had been afraid.

His head stirred on the pillows and his eyes opened. For a moment he looked at her, confused, and then his mouth twisted into a smile. 'Well, hello. You've given your protector the slip, I see.'

'A maiden has to have a little fun.' Gina smiled.

'And you can't have that with Struan?'

'She doesn't think so.' The deep voice behind her

made Gina jump, and Struan's hand came down on her shoulder. 'There's no fun for our Dr Buchanan. At least, not the sort I'm thinking of. She's already claimed, Lloyd. The lady has given her hand to our Wayne.'

'Wayne. . .' Lloyd's eyes creased in incomprehension and then widened as he realised what Struan meant. 'Not. . . Not Wayne Macky?'

'The very same,' Struan said morosely. 'She must have fallen for his waistcoats. And I might have been persuaded to sacrifice my beard, but donning a three-piece suit is asking too much of a man.'

'I'll say,' Lloyd said with feeling. He grinned up at Struan. 'I've been meaning to ask you about your beard.'

'It had a Christian burial last week. The lady didn't like it.'

'But. . .' Lloyd looked from Struan to Gina and back again, and shook his head in incomprehension. 'Gina, are you engaged to Wayne?'

'Yes.' Gina was glaring for all she was worth at Struan but it wasn't affecting him one bit.

'Then why. . .?' Lloyd fought for understanding. 'Then why get rid of the beard?'

'The lady's not married yet,' Struan said solemnly. 'And I read somewhere, he who dares, wins. So. . . My greatest sacrifice. My beard!'

Lloyd choked and for the first time Gina saw his young face crease into laughter. The defenceless look lifted and she almost forgave Struan his impudence. Almost.

Struan glanced at his watch. 'Six-fifteen. I'm running a bit late. There's things I've had to organise. Lloyd, can you cope with another visitor tonight?'

'Sure,' Lloyd said easily. 'I've had my mum and dad and brother this afternoon, but they're hardly tiring. Mum sits and knits, Dad watches the football on the telly and my brother chats up the nurses. Who's coming?'

'A friend.' Struan spread his hands. 'Lloyd, Greg Mace went through medical school with me. I thought you might like. . .' He hesitated

'I might like what?' Lloyd stared. Struan seemed suddenly unsure.

The ward door opened. Lloyd and Struan took no notice but Gina glanced behind. A big man, casually dressed in sweater and cord trousers and with an air of authority on his broad, good-natured face, glided across the smooth linoleum towards the bed. In a wheelchair

'Hi,' he said easily, spinning to a halt beside Lloyd's bed. He smiled across at Struan. 'Hell, Maitland! What happened to your facial growth? Did you forget to feed it?'

Struan turned and grinned. 'Greg,' he said softly, and there was real affection in his voice. He strode around to grip the newcomer's hand. 'Greg Mace. . . Dr Greg Mace, I'd like you to meet Lloyd and Gina.'

Doctor. . .

There was a long, long silence, while Lloyd assimilated what Struan had done. It seemed the whole world held its breath.

'Lloyd, I know it's much too soon,' Struan said eventually into the stillness, 'but this morning I thought about the one thing in all this that you were most afraid of. You're a doctor. A born doctor. And you're afraid you'll lose your medicine. I know that's not going to happen—regardless of the outcome—so I figured. . . Well, what's happened to Greg is the worst possible thing that can happen to you. If things go badly you'll end up in a wheelchair. Well, Greg was in a car accident in the final year of medical school. And it hasn't stopped him.'

Still silence. It could go any way, Gina thought

desperately. Lloyd could tell them to go to hell. He could imagine they were preparing him for paraplegia. She found herself gripping her palms almost to bleeding point. Let Struan be right. . .

Then Lloyd was nodding slowly. 'So. . . So you reckon I should face my worst fears and then get on with my life?' he said.

'Something like that.'

Lloyd took a deep breath. The boy had courage. It was written all over his face. He reached his hand down to take Greg's proffered grip.

'I'm. . .I'm pleased to meet you, then, sir.'

'Not so much of the sir.' Greg smiled. 'I'm not much more than ten years older than you.'

Lloyd nodded. There was a question forming in his mind. They could see it working across his face.

'Are you. . .? Have you gone into psychiatry?'

'Psychiatry?' Greg gave a booming laugh that made visitors to the neighbouring patients turn their heads. 'Hell, no. I'm a pathetic listener, always wanting to shove my oar in and give advice. I'd make a dreadful shrink.'

'Then, what. . .?'

'I'm a family doctor. I have a thriving practice twenty miles from here. One wife, three kids, two dogs, twenty chooks, five rabbits at last count, though Flossie's pregnant again so by the time I get home there might be six more, and one budgie. I should be helping my son fix the hen-house right at this very moment but Struan told me I was needed.' He sighed. 'So I knew I either came or suffered being fetched. Struan has such a nice way of getting what he wants.'

Lloyd smiled absently, his mind obviously in top gear. 'A. . .a country practice.'

'I wouldn't do anything else.' Greg smiled. 'I've wanted to practise medicine in the country since I was eight years old. The accident made me think a few things through, but so far. . . Well, so far I haven't had any real problems.'

'Like. . .' Lloyd grimaced, as though almost afraid to ask. 'Well, you wouldn't be able to deliver babies, would you?'

'Why the hell not?'

'Well, but. . .'

'I have a bit of trouble with the brakes on my wheelchair when I'm doing a forceps delivery,' Greg admitted. 'I've figured it only takes an extra nurse who handles my handles. She pulls me back when I tell her. Once you've got a well-trained assistant, the thing's a breeze.'

'But. . .'

'The only time I've ever been in real trouble was once when I was visiting an old patient whose home I knew was accessible. If the homes aren't, then the ambulance boys bring them in. Patients accept that. There's lots of districts where perfectly fit doctors refuse house-calls, and they know if they assure me of a ramp or no steps and a bit of room I'll come. Well, once I called in on an elderly patient and he took one look at me and dropped dead of heart failure. I had to fall out of the chair to give him CPR. Couldn't do a damned thing—it was his time to die—and there was nothing in the place solid enough to use to haul myself back into the chair. The phone was wall-mounted, out of reach. I spent hours contemplating a corpse before someone realised the doctor was missing and came to look.' He grinned. 'The good thing about being a country GP, though, is that there's always someone looking for you.'

'So. . .' Lloyd was staring down at Greg's chair, stunned. 'So it hasn't stopped you?'

'I can't ski any more,' Greg confessed. 'And I rarely operate. It's just too much bother. I do minor procedures, but the rest. . . Well, I never much wanted to be a surgeon anyway.'

'Me neither,' Lloyd grinned, and he gave Struan a black look. 'I helped Struan remove an appendix a few weeks back. I sewed up and he told me to enrol in a needlework course before I came back.' His smile faded and he looked up at Struan. 'You guessed, didn't you? What my worst fear was?'

'It stuck out a mile,' Struan told him. 'And me telling you wouldn't have helped. So Greg——'

'Was coerced,' his friend chuckled. 'Struan, are you and your lady-friend going out to dinner?'

'I. . .' Struan looked slightly taken aback. 'Well, yes. Eventually.'

'Then I suggest you go now,' Greg told him. 'I don't want to be late home and Lloyd and I have things to talk about. So if you don't mind. . .'

'You mean, shove off?'

'You got me here to talk to Lloyd,' Greg told him. 'So, yes. Shove off.'

The ward door closed behind them with a swish. To Gina's surprise, Struan didn't walk straight to the lifts. Instead he leaned against the wall, his shoulders sagged and he let his breath out in a long rush.

'It paid off,' Gina said gently, seeing the tension ease from his face.

'Yeah. . . It was a gamble, though.'

'He who dares, wins,' Gina repeated slowly, and Struan's face relaxed even further. His dark eyes creased into laughter.

'That's right, Dr Buchanan. I forgot. . .'

'I don't think you could forget. It's in your nature.'

'You sound disapproving, Dr Buchanan. Don't you think I should have asked Greg to come?'

Gina hesitated. If it had failed. . . If Lloyd had thought they were assuming he definitely was going to be paraplegic. . .

He hadn't, though. The risk had paid off, and Struan knew Lloyd well enough to guess it would have.

'No,' she said slowly. 'I don't. . .I don't disapprove.'

'So I can keep my motto?'

'I'm not sure.' The laughter hadn't faded from Struan's eyes and there was a gleam of something else there—the gleam of a man facing a challenge. 'It depends. . .'

'On whether I'm talking about you,' Struan nodded. 'Well, I am, Dr Buchanan. So put up your guard this minute. You're going to need it.'

'Then. . .' Gina took an uncertain breath. 'Then I think I'd better go back to the hotel.'

'But you're dressed for a night on the town.'

'Dinner,' Gina said desperately. 'That's all we agreed on. Dinner.'

'Then, dinner it is.' Struan turned and pushed the lift button, and then took Gina's hand in his with a decisive, strong movement. 'Not to take you at least to dinner would be an absolute waste. Waste not, want not,' he grinned. 'So I'll start with the waste not.'

'Struan. . .'

'Yes, my love?'

'I'm not your love.'

'Not yet. But I haven't done the waste not part yet.'

'I don't. . .'

The lift glided open before them. Three nurses looked out at them with interest. Struan smiled companionably and drew Gina inside.

'Our chariot,' he said in satisfaction. 'Gina, just shut up and let me take you to dinner. You never know, you might shock yourself to the core by really enjoying yourself.'

'Some hope,' she said acidly, but she whispered it, and her voice felt funny. The feel of her hand in his was doing all sorts of strange things to her.

'It is, isn't it?' He smiled down at her and his eyes

were caressing. They made her heart lurch within her. 'Some hope. A hope to cherish. A hope that all our dreams came true, Gina Buchanan. From this moment forth.'

He took her to Benedict's.

Benedict's. . . Maybe Melbourne's most elegant eating place, set in a vast stone mansion incongruously surrounded by streets of ordinary homes. Gina looked out doubtfully as the taxi drew to a halt. This wasn't her scene. These types of places—well, they were for people who didn't mind squandering money. . .

'Disapproval, my Gina?' Struan mocked as he helped her from the car.

'It's no less than I expected,' she retorted, and then bit her lip. Her words had been rude. Struan had brought her to Melbourne and was being good to her—in his own lights. The least she could do was to be gracious.

Struan looked down at her face. 'The least you can do is enjoy it,' he said, echoing her thoughts. 'Not look as if I'm forcing you to swallow prunes.'

'But. . .' Damn this man. She could keep nothing from him. She managed a smile. 'I'm sorry. It's just. . .I know it's expensive.'

'And I worked ninety or more hours last week, and we'll both probably do the same this week. Benedict's will give us a meal I can remember all the time I'm doing it. It's worth it. No matter what Wayne thinks.'

'Wayne wouldn't——'

'Bring you somewhere like this?' Struan said grimly. 'You don't have to tell me that. Now, take that teetotal look off your face this minute and enjoy yourself. This is your boss speaking, Gina Buchanan, and that's an order. Starting now!'

She looked up at his intent face, the glimmer of a smile just discernible behind the stern façade.

'Yes. . .yes, sir,' she whispered.

And in the end she did enjoy herself. The restaurant was so different from anywhere she had gone with Wayne that it was almost ludicrous. With its reputation, she had expected supercilious waiters and a menu she didn't understand. Instead they were greeted by a beaming hostess, who settled them into a welcoming corner like a chook making sure her chicks were comfortably bedded for the night. She went through the menu with them and then discreetly left them to themselves.

'Goat cheese soufflé. . .' Gina stared down at the table as their waiter departed, bearing his menus and the order. 'I don't believe I've just ordered goat cheese soufflé.'

'Don't you want it?'

Gina spread her hands. 'I. . .I haven't a clue. I hope I do.'

She did. As a taste treat it was sensational, and afterwards the crispy-skinned salmon and mouthwatering lemon tart made her feel that maybe Wayne was cheating himself by not splashing out just occasionally. She sipped her luscious wine and Struan watched her like some benevolent genie.

'Are you really so restricted in your eating places?'

Gina flushed. 'It's just that Wayne. . . Wayne. . .'

'You're a big girl now, Gina.' Struan smiled. 'Almost all grown-up. Do you really only eat where Wayne dictates?'

'I only go out with Wayne.'

'For heaven's sake, Gina. You're nearly thirty!'

'I am not! I'm twenty-nine next month.'

'Well, well. Nearly a birthday girl.' He smiled, and lifted the Sauterne from the cooler to refill her glass. 'Happy birthday for next month. Will we marry on your birthday?'

'Struan. . .' Gina took a desperate sip of her wine

and then wished she hadn't. The wine. . .the beautiful food. . .the dim lighting and the ambience of peace all around her was doing strange things to her heart. Almost. . . Almost making her agree with him. 'Struan, the joke's gone far enough,' she pleaded. 'I'm engaged to Wayne.'

'But you're not wearing his ring.'

'He. . .he hasn't given me one yet.'

'So wear mine.'

His hand slid into his trouser pocket and a small box of black velvet appeared in his palm. 'I'm not joking, my Gina,' he said gently. 'I've never been more serious in my life.' He flipped the lid to reveal a single exquisite diamond on a band of fine gold.

'I had some time to kill this morning.' He smiled at her. 'And I always shop when I'm bored. Odd, though. This morning there was only one thing in the whole damned city that I wanted to buy.'

There was a long, long silence. The whole world, it seemed, was holding its breath. The ring lay on its bed of velvet like the temptation of sin. The apple before Eve. . .

It would be so easy to lift her hand and take it. It would be so easy to look up into those laughter-filled eyes and succumb. . .

And then what? Happiness? Glorious, physical joy, as her mother had had with her father—for six short years?

And then heartbreak.

'Don't marry with your heart,' her mother had made her promise in the last few days of her illness. 'Take a good look at who you intend marrying and use common sense. Marry with your head, my Gina. Make yourself safe. . .'

Gina looked up at Struan and the agony must have shown in her face. He nodded, and the small box snapped shut.

'Maybe it's too soon to ask you to wear it.' His hands came over the table to clasp hers. 'But it's here, Gina. Ready whenever you are.'

'How. . .? How many other girls have you proposed to?' she whispered.

His smile deepened. 'Three,' he confessed. 'See, for you I expose my past.'

'Three. . .?'

'One at kindergarten. Melissa Dodds. She had the longest pigtails and the reddest hair-ribbons of any girl in the place. I was besotted. Then, when I was fifteen, I proposed to my science teacher. We all did. I think that's why I became a doctor—so I could spend more time in the biology lab with Miss Arthur supervising.'

'And the third. . .?'

His smile slipped a little. 'Well,' he said softly, 'Sara was a bit different. But everyone has a past. Even you have your Wayne. . .'

'That's right,' Gina said with astringency. 'I have Wayne. And, for all you patronise Wayne, he's a caring person, and he's my fiancé. I'll thank you to remember that, Struan Maitland. So I hope you bought that darned ring on a use or return basis—or maybe you'll just have to keep it for proposal number five.'

She took a deep breath. Whether Struan Maitland was stuck with a useless diamond ring was no concern of hers. It couldn't be. 'Can we go back to the hotel now?'

'Soon.' He didn't even seem disappointed. He was smiling reassuringly, his smile a caress.

He should still have his beard, Gina thought suddenly—desperately. It was at least a tiny barrier to that good-looking face—to those damned eyes. . .

'I've nearly finished my coffee,' he told her. 'Meanwhile. . .' He paused. 'Take that scared look off your face, Gina Buchanan. I've declared my intentions but I'm not the bullying type. You have at least a week before I start getting pushy. Meanwhile, if you weren't out buying engagement rings this morning, what did you do with your day?'

'I. . .' Gina fought for composure. Her heart was still thumping and his dark eyes were holding her hostage. What had she done?

Finally the mist cleared. Work. In concentrating on professional issues lay salvation. 'I. . .I went to see a friend of mine. A doctor I know from university. Elizabeth Chong.'

'Nice for you.'

'No.' She shook her head, remembrance of the morning flooding back, and her eyes suddenly brimmed with unshed tears. 'No, it wasn't, Struan.'

A waiter came and refilled their coffee-cups—unasked and unnoticed.

'Want to tell me why?'

She nodded, taking a gulp of coffee. She'd expected a near-empty cup, and the unexpected heat of the fresh coffee took her breath away. 'Jenny, Lisa's mum, came to Melbourne after having made an appointment to see Liz Chong a few weeks ago.'

Struan's face stilled. 'And?'

'And Liz diagnosed inoperable cancer. Cancer of the cervix. Multiple metastases with spread to the liver.'

Struan's face closed. The laughter died from his eyes. There was silence—long, uncomfortable and tragic.

'Dear God,' Struan said at last, and it was almost a prayer. 'Why. . .?' He stared at Gina. 'Why did she go to. . .Liz Chong, did you say? Did she know her?'

'It seems she picked her at random from the Melbourne phone book. A lady doctor who wouldn't have contacts with anyone in Gundowring. She used a false name.'

'So. . . How did you know?'

'I found her card in Jenny's drawer when I was finding the photograph for Lisa. So I telephoned. The receptionist had never heard of Jenny—so I took a photograph there this morning.'

'Why?' Struan's voice was intent, and so were his eyes. 'Why, for heaven's sake?'

'Because it's important for Lisa to know. Not now, maybe, but in the future. As far as Lisa's concerned, her mum deserted her. If Jenny had no choice—and her suicide was only pre-empting her death by a few weeks—then it'll make a difference to Lisa's memories.'

Struan's eyes flew up, and his look reflected sudden comprehension. 'You mean, she won't be scarred by desertion—like you.'

'I'm not scarred.'

'Like hell you're not,' he growled. Then his head dropped into his hands. 'Jenny. . .' His voice reflected anguish.

'She was your patient?'

'She was. But she'd hardly been near me for years, except for Lisa's trifling ailments. I remember giving her a hard time when she sprained her ankle twelve months ago because she wouldn't have a pap smear. She said she'd start when she was forty.'

'It might not have shown up then,' Gina said gently, hearing the self-blame in his voice. 'It sounds as if it was a really aggressive invasion.'

'But it might have shown. I should have insisted.'

'You can't force people to take regular health-checks.' Gina hesitated, and then put her hand out to cover his. There was still self-blame in Struan's voice—astonishing in someone who seemed to treat life as a cause for laughter.

'We would have found it at post mortem,' Struan said bitterly. His hand was still under hers—unresponsive. 'But she left a note. The way she'd organised Lisa made it quite clear that her death was suicide, and the means she used were obvious. Sandra was dead against a post mortem, and the coroner looked at the scene and agreed it was unnecessary. If you hadn't done the detective-work we'd never have known.'

'Well, maybe it wouldn't have mattered.'

Struan shook his head. 'You're right. It matters. Long-term it'll make things easier for Lisa.' He banged his hand down on the table. 'I should have known. She was losing weight. I asked her about it—but she said she'd been dieting. I told her not to be a bloody fool. Great, wise advice. . .'

'Struan, you can't blame yourself.'

'Can't I just?' he said bitterly. 'You just watch me.'

They left soon after. The bubble of laughter had gone out of the evening and Struan sat back against the soft upholstery of the taxi with his arms folded and his face grim.

This was a side of Struan Gina hadn't seen before. Tight with pain. Her heart wanted to reach out to him. Desperately she wanted to touch him—comfort him.

The bright lights of the hotel were impersonal and unwelcoming after the intimacy of the restaurant. Gina and Struan rode up to the fourteenth floor without saying a word.

Gina couldn't speak. She felt as if she was being torn in two.

They stopped by her door. Struan lifted the key from her fingers and opened the door for her. She should walk straight in and slam the door after her. Instead. . . Instead she was capable of no such thing. She walked slowly past Struan, and made no objection as he followed her.

The window of her bedroom looked out over the city, as far away as the West Gate Bridge rising in a smooth, sweeping curve over the Yarra. Cars flowed over it as a brightly lit moving ribbon. There are people in those cars, Gina thought inconsequentially. Ants.

Ants with lives of their own that have nothing to do with me.

Nothing had anything to do with her. No one.

She hadn't turned on the room-lights.

Neither had Struan. Maybe he'd left her? she thought fleetingly as she stared out of the window, but then his hands touched her shoulders and she knew that he was with her.

Of her. Not with her. For this moment. . . For this moment this man was her soul-mate. He had anguish of his own. She could heal that anguish with her body, and she could no more refuse him comfort than fly to the moon. Struan Maitland needed her—and she needed him. She needed him more than she had needed anyone in her whole life.

She hadn't needed people. . . Since her mother died, she hadn't needed anyone. . .

She didn't need Wayne. . .

Stop it, she told her weeping heart. Stop it. Stop analysing. Just hold. You don't need this man either. He needs you, and that's why. . . That's why you're going to turn in his arms and hold your face up to be kissed.

It was a kiss of absolute surrender. It had to be. There was nothing else for this moment but to do just that—surrender herself to a feeling that was so powerful that it wouldn't be contained.

He could feel it. Struan's hands held hers and his kiss deepened, deepened until she felt as though she was drowning in a sea of desire. She opened her lips to his and returned the kiss, her hands holding him against her as eagerly as he held her.

And then he paused. She felt his body stiffen and he drew back, his eyes looking down at her in the half-light.

'Gina. . . My love. . .'

'Struan. . .' It was a sigh of longing and of hope—

that somehow she could cross the barrier of pain and rebuild trust destroyed more than twenty years ago. A plea that in these arms she could rebuild faith.

He looked down at her for a long, long moment, and then he gave a long, shuddering sigh. He pulled her in to him, moulding her breasts to his chest.

'My Gina. . .' It was a vow.

Her mind was still working. Just. . . She forced out her only concern. 'Struan. . . Struan, I'm not. . .I'm not protected.'

Struan held her away from him in a lithe, fluid movement. His eyes widened. 'You're offering. . .?'

'I'm just. . .' It was hard to make her voice rise above a whisper. 'I'm just saying I'm not protected.'

He smiled down at her, and his smile was so tender that she wanted to weep. 'Then you'll have to agree to marry me, my love. I could cope with a baby or two. Or six. Our babies. . .'

'No!' A flash of fear. A flash of reason. 'Struan. . .'

'You mean. . .' A long pause. 'You mean, you'll make love to me but you won't marry me?'

'No. Yes!' She shook her head in miserable confusion. 'Struan, I don't know. Please, I don't know.'

There was a long, long silence and then Struan gathered her hands into his. He felt her tremble, and he swore almost silently to himself.

'Then I'll just have to convince you, Gina, my love. And I don't know any other way than taking you to my bed.'

'But. . .'

'But you're not protected.' He smiled suddenly and his white teeth gleamed. 'I'm a man equipped for emergencies, though.'

'You. . .you expected this?'

'Let's say I hoped.' He stooped suddenly and swept her up into strong arms. 'A man doesn't buy an engagement ring without hope. Let's just say I hoped like hell—I hoped more than anything on God's earth. And sometimes. . . Sometimes, Gina, my love. . . Sometimes miracles are allowed to happen, when you hope hard enough.'

He swept her triumphantly away from the window, striding back to lower her on to the vast bed. 'You slept in here all by yourself last night?' he asked, smiling tenderly down at her. 'What a waste.'

And then his smile faded and he placed a finger on her cheek, tracing the contours of her face down to her throat. 'You're sure about this, my Gina? It's not just a last fling before you marry our Wayne?'

She shook her head and then hesitated. 'Maybe. . . maybe it is,' she whispered. 'Would you mind?'

'If you still marry Wayne I'll mind like mad,' he told her. He was unbuttoning his shirt as he spoke and the sight of his bare muscled torso in the moonlight made Gina gasp. And ache. . .

'But for now. . .' The remainder of his clothes disappeared and he knelt with a soft sigh of triumph and gathered her close against his nakedness. 'For now, Wayne doesn't exist. Neither does the past, my lovely, lovely Gina. For tonight. . . For tonight, you're mine.'

You're mine. . .

Gina drifted in a cloud of unreality as his fingers removed her blouse. Vaguely she felt herself helping him, eager to rid herself of the last barrier between them. He felt so good. His skin. . . She wanted to be closer to this man than she had ever been. She wanted to be one. . .

She looked into the depths of his eyes and knew that, for now, there was no need to want. For now. . . For this moment, they were one. One being. One love. . .

'Struan,' she whispered. 'Oh, Struan. . .'

His eyes held her, loved her, exulted in her loveliness.

'My Gina,' he whispered back. 'My love.'

And then she was gathered to him and their bodies were merging in a mist of loving surrender. This was right. This was how it should be—now and forever.

Her hands clung to him, pulling him closer, closer, as he took her to peaks of tenderness she had never dreamed of. And even the pain—the small, sharp stab that she had half expected—was part of the glory. Part of the conversion of Gina Buchanan into a woman. A woman cherished. . .

CHAPTER EIGHT

GINA woke with the dawn.

She was cocooned in a sea of warmth and protection—cradled against Struan as though she was where she belonged. Struan Maitland had claimed his woman and his hold told the world he intended to keep her.

Gina's eyes widened. She stared out at the dawning Melbourne sky and felt the first stirring of panic. And then the second.

And then it wasn't just a stirring. Blind panic washed over her in waves.

Dear God, what had she done? What. . .?

She flinched away from Struan's touch and Struan's hold tightened, even in sleep. She was naked against him, her back curved into his chest. Skin against skin. . .

It had been so good. It had been like nothing she had dreamed of.

It had been with the wrong man. She was engaged to be married to Wayne Macky. . .

She pulled against Struan's constricting hold like a rabbit caught in a trap. Fear. . . She had fought so hard to stay independent. She had fought to allow nothing like this ever to happen to her. And in one night. . . In one crazy night she had forgotten everything—the promise she had made to her mother—the vow she had given to Wayne—everything.

Struan was awake now, his arms tightening their hold rather than loosening as she struggled.

'Going somewhere?' His voice was slurred with sleep.

'Please, Struan. . .'

He caught the fear in her voice and was suddenly wide awake. His arms released her and he sat up, the bedclothes falling away to reveal his naked chest. 'What's wrong, my lovely. . .?'

'I'm not your lovely anything.' Gina's voice rose on the edge of hysteria. 'Struan, I'm not. I don't. . .I don't know. . .'

'You don't know why you let me make love to you,' he finished for her. His hands came up to take her bare smooth shoulders and his hold sent a shudder right through her. 'And you were a virgin,' he said softly. 'A virgin, my Gina. . .'

'Double bonus for you,' Gina said bitterly, and then wished she hadn't at the blaze of anger in his eyes.

'What's that supposed to mean?'

'I don't know.' It was a wail of despair. She pulled away from him and rose, and then gasped as the bedclothes fell away to reveal her naked body. She made a grab for the sheet and he let her have it, but in covering herself she exposed him.

'Struan, I didn't want to let you make love to me.'

'Your memory's not so good.' His eyes were watchful—wary—as though he didn't know where she intended going. As if she could go anywhere like this. . . 'Gina, I didn't make love to you last night. *We* made love. You and I, Gina. You wanted me as much as I wanted you, and I'm damned if I'm letting you tell yourself that I seduced you.'

'But. . .'

'But I didn't.' He rose then, moving like a lean and powerful panther, striding across the room to take her in his arms. He kissed her on the hair and his hands moved beneath her protective sheet. 'We did. So now. . . Now you have to face Wayne and tell him you've made a mistake.'

'Struan, I might have made a mistake,' Gina whispered. 'But not with Wayne.'

Dead silence. Then Gina was moving away from him, backing towards the bathroom.

'Please,' she whispered. 'Struan, you have to give me some room.' She put her hand to her face in a gesture of fear. 'I don't know what to do. Dear God, I don't know what to do.'

'You might try trusting me.'

'I can't.' She paused, her hand on the bathroom door.

'Why not?'

'Because. . . Because you threaten me. You're not safe. With you. . .'

'Your life would be unpredictable. Exciting, even. We could do so much, you and I, my lovely Gina, if only you could find the courage.'

'I don't want an exciting life,' she said miserably. 'I want security.'

'And you reckon our Wayne will give you that?'

'He'd love me.'

'But you've betrayed him,' Struan said easily. He crossed to his clothes and started dressing. 'How are you going to explain last night to Wayne—or aren't you? Is he still going to expect his virgin bride?'

Gina's face flushed to the roots of her hair. 'I can't——'

'Can't tell him?' Struan shook his head. 'Not only that. You can't marry him, Gina. Not feeling how you're feeling. You want me as much as I want you, and regardless of whether you agree to marry me, you can't agree to live with Wayne.'

'Surely that's up to Wayne. . .'

'Gina. . .' Struan was half-dressed, in trousers and unbuttoned shirt. He came across the room and held Gina's shoulders. Gina clutched her bedsheet for all it was worth—attempting to put some sort of barrier between them. 'Gina, what you are trying to find with Wayne can be found in a thousand other ways.

Someone who'll be there with total dependability for as long as he lives. Someone who won't threaten you or ask you to do anything you might not like, and someone who won't walk out on you. Believe it or not, you have it in me, but you don't believe that. Some day—some time soon—it'll dawn on you that you can trust me—that I'm not as dangerous as you think. Even if it means me selling my damned motorbike I'll persuade you. But for now. . . For now, you have to replace Wayne with something else that will do all he will. A stuffed soft toy springs to mind—as something a bit more cuddly and just as boring.'

'You're not fair. . .'

'No. But I'm in love, my Gina. All's fair in love and war, and this is both. I'm fighting for you.'

He left her then, going back to his own room to shower, change and breakfast. She needed him to go, and he accepted that. Gina had the look of a hunted animal, and only the cruel would keep hunting.

He wasn't cruel, Gina acknowledged as she stood for too long under the streaming shower. She didn't know what the heck he was.

Afterwards they formally booked out of their hotel, sent the luggage ahead to the airport and then spent the morning at the hospital, with a Lloyd who had cheered immeasurably since they'd last seen him. The physiotherapist was with him when they arrived and they watched the careful massage of limp limbs.

'They won't stay limp, though,' Lloyd promised. 'It's odd how facing the worst head-on makes the worst seem less likely.'

'Greg made you face the worst?' Struan asked the boy on the bed. Gina had subsided to silence. She sat in the armchair provided for visitors and tried to concentrate, but she couldn't make herself ask questions.

'If you could call it the worst,' Lloyd agreed. 'Greg

went over every problem he's met, practising medicine as a paraplegic, and showed me how each one could be overcome. Finally, though. . . Finally he told me he's had no feeling whatsoever from the waist down ever since his accident. And I can feel a lot. So. . . Well, the physiotherapist has been encouraging too. She reckons it might take six months but I'll be back on my feet eventually.'

'It might be even longer than that,' Struan warned.

'Yeah, well. . .' Lloyd smiled shyly at Gina. 'For as long as it takes. You don't have to hold my job until then, though.'

'I'll enjoy doing it.' Gina smiled back, her face brighter than her mind. She was starting to think that escape from Gundowring might be the easiest solution to this mess all around. She couldn't go, though. Not after all Lloyd had done for her. 'I'll stay for however long it takes.'

They ate lunch in the hospital cafeteria. Struan wanted to go to the park but Gina refused. She wanted people around her. She wanted a buffer.

The plane was due to leave at four. Three long hours to go.

'Look, I have business I could be doing instead of sitting staring at polystyrene cups,' Struan said at last. 'And I've a feeling that with me gone you might be tempted to take yourself for a walk out by the river. Is it OK if I meet you at the airport at three-thirty?'

The relief was overwhelming. Gina lifted grateful eyes to Struan and he gave a rueful grin.

'As ogreish as that, am I?'

Gina shook her head but didn't speak. She didn't trust herself.

'Well, off you go, then.' He leaned over and kissed her lightly on the head. 'A nice long walk and a think about marital bliss with Wayne's waistcoat. See you later, Dr Buchanan.'

And he was gone, striding easily through the mill of people in the cafeteria. He looked. . . He looked almost as though he was humming!

Insensitive toad! Gina thought desperately. How could he not see how miserable she was?

He did see. And he offered a solution.

Some solution. Marriage with Struan Maitland—a man who had the capacity to break her heart.

That was what it was, she accepted drearily as she did as she was ordered—walked slowly along the river-bank, not fast enough to worry her healing thigh, and watched the Sunday crowds enjoy themselves. She wanted to marry Wayne because Wayne couldn't stir her to the pain Struan could inflict.

Struan wouldn't hurt her. Not intentionally.

How could she know that? Her mother had taken a gamble and the gamble had failed. So Gina had promised her mother that she wouldn't be as foolish. So. . .

So stop being so darned foolish, Gina Buchanan, she told herself. Get your life into order.

She couldn't marry Wayne. . . Not after. . .

No. She couldn't. Last night she had broken her pledge to Wayne and, whatever happened, she couldn't undo that. It wasn't fair to Wayne to go ahead and marry him.

Perhaps, he wouldn't care. . .

'He'd care that you slept with Struan!'

She spoke out loud, and an elderly lady with two matched poodles on pink leads stopped promenading and stared. Gina talked on, oblivious.

'He'd only care because you actually slept with him. He wouldn't be jealous of the emotional side. . . Because he's as emotional as a stuffed fish!'

Despite the poodles, Gina gave a choked giggle. For

the first time in her life she saw Wayne clearly, as he really was—not some rescuer who had kept her sanity, but a stuffy, conscientious man who had fulfilled his obligation to her out of love of routine, obligation to duty and the need to be seen as charitable.

'Oh, Wayne. . .' She bit her lip. 'How am I going to tell you?'

Well, not by announcing that she was in love with Struan Maitland, that was for sure. She shook her head and moved on. Reluctantly, the poodle promenade and Gina parted company.

'I don't have to.' The decision descended with the surety of good sense. 'Struan Maitland is just like your father. You can resist him if you keep your head. You tell Wayne you've made a mistake, you fulfil your obligations to the hospital until Lloyd is back, and then you return to city practice. You don't need a man, Gina Buchanan. You know that.'

She knew that. So why did the future seem so darned bleak?

She arrived at the airport early. Wayne had trained her well, she thought, as she settled herself into a chair with a magazine.

The magazine held her concentration for all of three seconds.

Who in heaven's name cared about who was sleeping with who in social circles—or the latest fad diet? She threw the magazine aside restlessly, her mind homing straight back to Struan.

This was impossible. She had months to go—months of professional practice where Struan Maitland had to be an associate and nothing more. Nothing more. . .

A slurpy kiss landed joyfully on the back of her neck. Uuurgh! What on earth. . .?

Gina twisted in her chair, almost reluctant to see what—or who—was doing the kissing. When she saw, though, her face broke into a delighted smile. A golden Labrador puppy, about eight weeks old, was wriggling ecstatically in Struan Maitland's grasp. As Gina turned the pup wriggled forward and repeated the kiss, this time straight on her nose.

'What the——?' Gina burst into laughter and the wriggling bundle somehow landed on her lap. 'Oh, for heaven's sake. . . Oh, you gorgeous thing!'

The puppy agreed with her. It bounded up and planted another moist greeting—and another. Gina fended him off, but it was like trying to control the movements of a tin of worms. A tubby tin of worms. She grabbed him and held, and then looked up into Struan's laughing eyes.

'Whose. . .? For heaven's sake, Struan. . . Whose is the puppy?'

'Yours.'

'Mine!' Gina took a deep breath. She looked from Struan to pup, and then back again. 'You can't be serious?'

'Look.' Struan smiled and drew a sheaf of papers from his top pocket. 'Registration papers for Rebuck Mardinka Royal. That's him. Wacky for short, though. . .'

'Wacky?'

'Wacky because he's a substitute for Wayne Macky. Much nicer, though, and infinitely more huggable. Here are the registration papers, made out in your name—Dr Gina Buchanan, Gundowring Hospital, Gundowring. Short of legal adoption, we can't get any more official that this.'

'But. . . But I don't want a puppy!'

'Don't you?' Struan stood back, watching her. 'It seems to me that's exactly what you do want. Something loyal, dependable, lovable. Wacky, here, supplies everything you have in Wayne, bar the waistcoat. And there's even some cute doggy ones of those—though I suspect Wacky might tear them into shreds in seconds.'

'Oh, Struan. . .' Gina stared up at him through a mist of tears. 'For heaven's sake. . .'

'You said that before,' he said kindly. 'You need to get original. Now, Gina Buchanan, I've gone to a great deal of trouble to obtain this here dog. I contacted the Kennel Council and four breeders before finding someone with a suitable pup to sell, and then I had to persuade them I was a noble, dog-loving fellow of impeccable credentials before they'd let me near him. There's a pet transporter outside with the meter ticking. If you decide you don't want him, then I pop him back in the transporter and he's off back home, to be sold to someone who knows a great little dog when they see one. So, instead of saying, "For heaven's sake," you need to decide. You have a dog, Gina Buchanan. Will you keep him?'

A dog. . .

Gina looked down at the wriggling, joyous bundle in her arms and her mind went back to the dog she had killed. The night she met Struan. . .

When she had told Struan she didn't want a dog it had been a lie. A child moving from foster-home to foster-home was never permitted a pet, though, and at university and training hospitals there had never been room. She had a vague memory of a dog when her father was around—but none since then. Now. . .

'Would they let me keep him in my hospital flat?' she asked, and Struan grinned.

'Try asking the chairman of the hospital board.' He drew his hand over his face, his grin disappearing as he did. 'Well, Dr Buchanan, we have considered your request, and as long as you're prepared to pay for reinforcing the vegetable-garden fence we've decided to accede to your request to house your noble animal.

We even think the nursing home residents will be besotted.'

'I can keep you. . .' Struan's laughing face was ignored. There was light at the end of Gina's lonely tunnel, in the form of one wriggling pup. Wacky. . . Her face fell. 'I can't take him on the plane.'

'All organised. There's a container waiting at Reception. It'll cost you, though.'

'You're not paying?'

'He's your pup.' Struan put his hand fleetingly on Gina's head. 'My gift, but from here on he's your responsibility, Gina Buchanan. One of those things you're so desperate to avoid.'

'I don't. . .I don't run from responsibility.' It was hard to talk when Wacky was trying to help.

'No. Maybe you don't. You run from commitment, though, because you're so scared of pain. Well, maybe Wacky's the start of showing you that the joy's worth the risk.'

Wayne was waiting as they emerged from the airport terminal at Gundowring. Sunday afternoon, Gina thought fleetingly, and he's still wearing his waistcoat. Funny how she had never seen it as inappropriate before. It was just Wayne. Part of the dependability.

Struan had fallen behind. 'I'll bring the luggage,' he'd grinned, as Gina had scooped her pup from his container. Wacky had been incarcerated for a whole two hours and he was showing Gina that it had felt like a lifetime. She was having the greatest difficulty holding him. She put him down on his lead, and as Wayne approached he started turning concentric circles around her legs.

'What on earth have you got?'

There was no mistaking Wayne's disapproval. It washed over her before his kiss of greeting landed on her cheek.

'A pup.' Gina grinned, twisting herself out of a knot of leather lead. 'Wacky, to be precise.' She smiled up at Wayne. 'Isn't he gorgeous?'

'Wacky. . .'

Whether Wayne meant his repetition of the pup's name to be a greeting was unsure, but Wacky took it as such. Excitedly he leapt up on to Wayne's immaculately trousered leg, but the excitement on top of confinement was too much for his distended bladder. A small stream trickled downward, right over the gleaming leather of Wayne's shoes.

'Bloody hell. . .' Wayne stared down with horror, and then, before Gina could realise what he was doing, he lifted his shoe and kicked. Hard.

The puppy flew about three feet, to land in a whimpering crumpled heap by the side of the path.

'Wacky!' Gina gave a whisper of horror as she fell to her knees. The pup whimpered in her hands. He crawled on to her knee and looked up fearfully, exuberance knocked right out of him. His first taste of the real world. . .

'How. . .? How could you. . .?' Gina's voice was a thread. 'Wayne, he's eight weeks old. . .'

'He peed on my shoe!'

'You kicked him.' Gina's fingers were running over the dog, feeling for broken bones. The puppy whimpered again and huddled closer.

'And I'll kick him again if he repeats the performance,' Wayne said grimly. 'Whose is it, for Pete's sake?'

'He's mine.'

Around them, Gina's fellow passengers were streaming past, out into the sun. Relatives were being greeted and there were tearful farewells too, as the passengers for the flight's next leg prepared for boarding.

There might just as well have been silence, though. There was Wayne, staring disgustedly down at Gina and the puppy crouched at his feet. A silent triangle, each caught up in horror.

'I'm not having a dog,' Wayne said finally, flatly. 'Not in my house.'

'My' house. . . Not 'our' house.

Gina closed her eyes. 'I'm sorry, then, Wayne. But I own a dog.'

'Don't be a bloody fool.'

Her eyes flashed open. 'I'm not a fool, Wayne.'

'After all I've done for you. . .'

Gina shook her head. 'Wayne, I'm. . .I'm grateful for all you've done for me. I am. But I think. . .I think gratitude's no basis for a marriage.'

'Not if you intend to keep dogs, it's not.' Wayne spread his hands. 'Look, let's just dump the thing down at the pound and get on with our lives. This is ridiculous.'

'Yes,' Gina whispered. 'This is ridiculous.' She stood up unsteadily, the pup clasped tightly to her. 'This whole engagement is ridiculous. If you'd given me a ring I could hand it back now, Wayne, but you didn't. So all I can say is—goodbye.'

There was a long, long silence. Finally an elderly lady jostled Wayne with her suitcase and he seemed to come down to earth.

'That's your decision?' he said flatly.

'Yes.'

'Then, that's all there is to it,' he said grimly. 'I never thought you'd be fool enough to give up security for a dog!' And he turned and walked swiftly to the car park.

'Thus endeth one engagement.'

Gina turned slowly, to find Struan watching from a few feet away. How long he'd been there, she didn't know.

'He hurt my dog,' she said flatly, lifelessly, and turned away. 'My puppy. I'll get a taxi into town.'

'Taxis aren't allowed to take dogs unless they're in cartons in the luggage compartment.'

'Well, I'm not putting him into any luggage compartment.'

Struan smiled. 'He'll be OK, you know, Gina. Puppies are tough. Like kids.'

'If I had a kicked child I wouldn't put him in a cardboard box in the luggage compartment either.' She sighed. 'I'll just have to walk.'

'It's a mile into town and you've a sore hip. I'll give you a lift.'

Gina gritted her teeth. Her resolve had been to stay aloof. It had worked for a whole two minutes.

'I'd appreciate that,' she said stiffly.

'Very sensible.' His dark eyes flashed humour as he sensed her reluctance, and he took her arm and guided her across to the car park.

'Where. . .where are our suitcases?'

'I sent 'em before us by taxi. I put my case in the side-car to get here, but I can't fit two suitcases, two people and one pup on the Harley.'

'The Harley. . .' Gina stopped dead. 'You mean, you're expecting me to travel by motorbike?'

'Lots of the nicest people do.' He smiled, and his arm kept right on propelling.

'But. . . But the pup. . .'

'Will be fine in the side-car, as long as you hold him.'

'Struan, I won't go.' Her voice rose in panic. To get on to a bike with this man. . .

'I'm not raping you, Gina.' Struan's voice was suddenly annoyed. 'I'm giving you a lift home.'

'I've never——'

'I know,' he interrupted her. 'You've never done anything that's the least bit scary. Life for Dr Gina Buchanan has been a process of finding security. Well, security has more than one aspect, my love.' He paused for a moment and the grip on her hand tightened. 'Just because you've thrown Wayne over and are about to ride on a motorbike it doesn't mean you've sacrificed security. In fact, it might be the opposite.'

They were staring down at the gleaming black and silver of his bike. It was as if Gina almost expected it to leap at her. This man. . . This bike. . . This situation. . .

'I can't take Wacky without someone holding him,' Struan told her. 'And that someone's you, my Gina. There's a spare helmet here.' He unlocked and flicked up a saddle-box. 'Put it on and let yourself go. For once in your life, Gina Buchanan, expect to enjoy yourself.'

Enjoy. . .

How was she supposed to enjoy the feeling of freedom the machine gave her? To sit with the wind on her face, her long blonde hair streaming out behind and the pup huddled warmly on her lap. . .

It was a feeling that frightened the life out of her, and it wasn't fear of accidents or dying that was scaring her half to death. It was fear of what was happening to her.

CHAPTER NINE

I<small>T WAS</small> a blessed relief to close the door of her hospital flat behind Struan Maitland. Relief. . .

So much had happened so fast. Things had changed as fast as the ribbon of road had moved under their feet as the huge motorbike brought her home. Safely, as he'd promised.

Why had she been so frightened?

She didn't have a clue. Other people weren't as afraid as Gina.

Other people didn't know as much as Gina about having things—people—snatched from them. Other people worked on a theory of invincibility.

Not everyone. . .

Lisa.

Struan was doing his ward-rounds now, but Lisa was Gina's patient. Her only one until she started work officially tomorrow.

Gina's pup seemed to have recovered from his trauma. He was down on the floor, sniffing his new home with wary interest. On impulse Gina scooped the little dog up and walked through to the children's ward.

The sister met her at the door. 'Oh, Dr Buchanan. I'm so glad you're back——' And then she stopped short as she saw what Gina was carrying. 'A dog. . .'

'A very small dog,' Gina smiled. 'Almost not a dog at all, Sister. If anyone was to accuse you of, say, letting animals into the hospital, you could tell them it looked like a fur muff.'

'A fur muff with a wet nose and wriggling tail?' Sister grinned, but spread her hands in a gesture of granting benevolence. 'It's not me who'll be stopping you, though, Doctor. Lisa's our only patient and the pup might help.'

'Problems?'

'She hasn't talked since you left. She's been walking—going to the toilet when she needs to—but she hasn't talked.'

Gina sighed. 'Not even to her aunt?'

'Sandra hasn't been in. She rang and said she was too busy this weekend.'

Gina's hands clenched in anger and the pup squirmed. 'Drat the woman.'

'I think. . .I think whatever decision we make about Lisa might have to exclude her aunt,' the nurse said sadly. 'It doesn't seem to be working.'

'No.'

Gina walked over to Lisa's bed. The child was a miserable hump under the bedclothes. She didn't emerge as Gina approached.

'Hi.'

No response.

'Lisa, I'd like you to meet Wacky.'

The silence was deafening.

Gina hesitated, and then placed Wacky on the bed-clothes. Sister would have a fit. . .

Lisa still didn't emerge.

Wacky wasn't a pup to be ignored. He could sense something under the bedclothes. His tail gave an excited wag, his nose went down and he wuffled forth, stalking this exciting prey.

A heap of tousled curls showed above the top sheet, but nothing else. That was a starting point. The damp nose went down and burrowed. Wacky emerged once, dragging Sam Tiger to the surface, but he obviously decided there was more exciting prey further down. Down he went again. Deeper. Deeper, until there was only a golden tail, wagging against the curls.

The bedclothes wriggled all by themselves as the nose went deeper.

Then child and pup exploded from the sheets in a mass of wriggling arms, legs and tail. Lisa's eyes were red-rimmed from crying, but they were incredulous now. The puppy was intent on licking her to death.

'Ooooh. . .' It was a child's cry of delight and Gina grinned. Joy. . . A glimpse of joy.

Gina sat down and gathered the pup to her before he precipitated his tubby self over the edge of the bed, and then put her spare arm round Lisa and hugged hard. 'You like my new pet?'

'Is he yours?' Lisa lifted a hand for Wacky to lick. 'Oh, Dr Buchanan. . .' Then her little face crumpled and she subsided. 'I thought. . .I thought you weren't coming back.'

'I told you I'd be back tonight,' Gina said sternly. She lifted the child's woebegone face to meet her eyes. 'Didn't I, Lisa?'

'I didn't believe you.'

No. Of course not. The promise had been one of an adult to a child who'd just suffered the ultimate betrayal.

'Well, I came.' Gina hugged her again. 'I have to. I start work here tomorrow—permanently—and my puppy has to get used to his new home.'

'Home?'

'Here. He's going to live here at the hospital with me.'

'With me too?'

'Well, while you're in hospital.'

The child's eyes fell away and she shifted. 'But I don't live here.'

'No,' Gina said softly. 'You don't. . .'

Say something reassuring about foster-care, she thought frantically. Say something. . .

It could be OK. It could. . .

Only if they found Lisa's father and he agreed to long-term care. . . No family would take Lisa to their hearts if they thought she would be snatched away. No one exposed themselves voluntarily to so much pain.

They'd love her. Any foster-family would love her. Gina had just been unlucky.

They'd love her but she wouldn't belong.

Lisa had slid off Gina's lap and sunk back on to her pillows. It was as if she wanted to disappear into their whiteness. Wacky gave her nose an encouraging lick but Lisa didn't have the heart even to push the pup away.

Now what? Inspiration, Dr Buchanan, Gina ordered herself, but all she felt was hopelessness. An awful, awful feeling of *déjà vu* was threatening to overwhelm her.

She looked around the ward—cheerful enough for a children's ward, but no place for a child whose only problem was loneliness and grief. The other beds were empty. The lone nurse was separated from her small patient by a glass partition and she was busy with bookwork. The beds were clinically white and sterile. Well, they were sterile apart from a couple of smudged puppy paw-marks which Gina hoped no one would notice. . .

Inspiration. . .

An idea was slowly forming, and it went against everything she had ever been taught.

A good doctor retained some professional detachment, no matter how concerned he or she might be. A good doctor. . .

She was just about to be a very bad doctor, then, because she couldn't bear to be otherwise. Gina left pup and child and walked swiftly over to the sister's station.

'Could we arrange for Lisa to stay with me?' she asked.

The nurse looked up, her eyes wide. 'With you. . .?'

'In my flat.' Gina motioned to Lisa. 'This is no place for her.'

'Social Welfare are coming on Friday. We thought. . . Well, when her aunt rang, she said the sooner we organised foster-care the better,' the nurse said.

'Maybe. But that still means another week in hospital. . .' Gina hesitated. The door through to her flat was just down the corridor from the sister's station, and that door led straight into Gina's living-room. 'What if we put her on my lounge-room couch? It's big, squishy with age, and looks the very place for a recuperating child. She can have the television and books, and she can have the puppy with her for company.'

'And you'd look after her?' The nurse was staring at Gina as though she had taken leave of her senses. Professional detachment was instilled in nurses too.

'I'm working in the hospital as of tomorrow morning. But if we put a barrier across the bottom of the door to stop the pup getting into the hospital we could leave the door open. Then she could be checked almost as constantly as she is now.'

'She'll be lonely.'

'Maybe. But she can get herself drinks, and food from my refrigerator if she wants it, and not have her temperature taken because it's hospital rules, and she can make a mess and play with the pup. . .'

'I don't know what Dr Maitland would say,' the girl said doubtfully.

'Lisa's my patient.' Gina flashed anger for a moment. She took a breath. 'If you agree to the checks. . .I can't take her unless you do.'

'What about tonight?'

'I'll take her now.'

'But you won't want checks tonight?'

'No. I don't start work until nine tomorrow.'

'I could go off duty.' The girl grinned. 'Wow, Dr Buchanan. I'd even be in time to share fish and chips with my kids and my husband. They told me they were having them when I came on duty and I was jealous.'

'Where do you get fish and chips?'

'Steve's Café. A block down from the hospital. Best greasies this side of Melbourne.'

'Then Lisa and I will have fish and chips too.' Gina smiled. 'It sounds great.'

It was a far cry from Benedict's.

Gina and Lisa ate fish and chips from newspaper while Wacky ate puppy-food at their feet. Afterwards they watched a funny/sad movie, curled up on the old sofa together, until Lisa and Wacky fell fast asleep.

Gina rose reluctantly to clear the mess. What had happened to her nice, ordered life? she wondered as she picked up dog-bowl and chewed socks and then started on the dishes. She looked over to the sofa and a reluctant smile played around her mouth. What a weekend! She'd had a proposal of marriage, lost her virginity, lost a fiancé and gained a pup.

And a child.

You haven't gained Lisa, insisted the voice inside her head. She's a patient.

'No.' Gina shook her head and splashed her dishes into the sink. Lisa wasn't a patient. Patients didn't pull on heartstrings like Lisa did.

You'll do more harm than good by letting her form an attachment to you, said that inner voice.

'She can hardly do that in a week.'

She's already done it.

'Damn!' Gina sloshed more water about until she felt better. Then she checked her pages of puppy instructions, settled Wacky in the laundry with clock and hot water bottle, as per orders, showed Wacky the instructions, answered the knock on the door and accepted Night Sister's complaint that the noise was disturbing patients, showed Wacky the instructions again, and finally put the puppy back on the sofa with Lisa. Lisa rolled over, put her arm around the pup, and both pup and child settled into deep sleep.

'What have I started here?' Gina looked down at child and dog and felt a stab of disquiet. Domesticity which couldn't continue?

You're leaving here as soon as Lloyd gets back, she reminded herself. You've never put down roots before, Gina Buchanan. Don't start now.

Another knock on the dividing door between the hospital and her flat disturbed the silence. Gina sighed. Now what? She had her charges quiet, and all she wanted was her bed. She flung the door wide, to be met by Struan.

She stepped back a pace. Struan was in doctor mode—his jeans and checked shirt of the afternoon now covered with a white coat.

'Go away,' Gina said tightly. 'I'm going to bed.'

'That's not what you said last night.'

'Struan. . .'

'I know. I know.' He flung his hands up in mock-defence. 'You want to forget last night ever happened. Not possible, Gina, love. But, as it happens, I'm not here to sweep you off your feet yet again. I need help.'

'You need help?'

'Hard as that might be to comprehend,' He smiled, but his smile didn't quite reach his eyes. 'Gina, I've a three-year-old boy in Casualty. His parents called an hour ago, wanting a house-call. He has a temp of forty-one, he's been vomiting for four hours continuously and his neck's stiffening while I watch. I've given penicillin intramuscularly as a precaution, before we brought him in. . . But I'd like you to see him.'

'Meningitis?' Gina's mind snapped back from personal troubles into work mode.

'I'm not sure. He's had a cold, and his mum says he had a fall this morning—but the combination. . .'

'Can't be ignored,' Gina agreed.

'I've explained to his parents the need for a lumbar puncture,' Struan told her. 'If you can come now. . .'

As if on cue the charge sister appeared down the hospital corridor.

'I'll keep an eye on Lisa, Doctor,' she assured Gina. 'At least, I will as long as that beast we've been hearing caterwauling down the hospital corridors doesn't turn vicious.'

Gina grinned and looked at the sofa. Lisa and Wacky were almost nose to nose—comforting each other in sleep. Incredibly unhygienic, but the best therapy Lisa could possibly have. 'You'll have to be careful,' she agreed. 'You should see what that savage mongrel can do to a sock!'

'You have Lisa in there?' Struan raised incredulous eyebrows as he looked into the living-room. 'Gina. . .'

'We should go.' Gina wasn't in the mood to discuss the rights and wrongs of her decision to take Lisa's care on herself. Not when there was a child possibly suffering from meningitis. 'Where is he?'

'In Casualty.' With a visible wrench Struan turned from the sight of the entwined pair on the sofa. A nod to Sister and he was striding down the corridor, Gina struggling to maintain his speed.

'I didn't think you were on duty,' she managed.

'No. Lesley is, but she's coping with a difficult labour so she asked me to do the house-call.'

'Busy little hospital,' Gina murmured.

'Busier than I'd like at the moment.' Struan dug his hands deep in his pockets.

'There's more?'

'I've an elderly lady in Ward Three—one of our

nursing home patients—who looks like she's just had a left-sided stroke. I should be assessing her now.'

'Is there someone else who can help me?' A possibility of meningitis meant a lumbar puncture—something which required either two doctors or a doctor and a very skilled nurse. To perform an intricate procedure on a wriggling child. . .

'No. Martin's out at the local speedway, and if he comes back in now they'll have to cancel the meeting. Rules. Doctor or else. And Rod's not confident of the procedure.'

'So it's you and me?'

'Mostly you, I'm afraid,' Struan told her. 'Lumbar punctures on three-year-olds are the province of paediatricians. I just intend to hold your hand.'

'Or hold his,' Gina said sharply.

The child was sick.

There was no mistaking the signs of major illness. Gina was often amused by parents who brought struggling, screaming children into the surgery and explained how ill they were, or how much pain little Tess or Ben was in. The trouble always seemed to be inversely proportional to the amount of noise made. As a rule, Gina had been taught to worry about the quiet ones. The rule hardly ever let her down.

And she needed to worry about Jack. . .

Jack Messer was huddled on his mother's lap, intermittently whimpering. His pudgy limbs were floppy as he lay in his mother's arms, and he didn't look around as Gina and Struan entered. He was in his own little hell of pain. Gina's heart sank when she saw him.

'Mr and Mrs Messer, this is Dr Buchanan, our new paediatrician,' Struan told the parents, his voice assuring them that their son was in capable hands. He knelt so that he was in Jack's gaze. 'Jack, this is our new lady doctor, who's really good at looking after little boys.'

Really good. . . Gina didn't feel it. She never felt good looking at a child as sick as this. The parents were mute with fear. They seemed to be farmers—both were wearing overalls and gum-boots, as though the little boy's illness had swept up unawares.

'He was OK at lunch-time,' the woman whispered, cementing Gina's suspicions.

Gina put her hand on Jack's forehead and winced.

'I think we'll prepare barrier nursing, regardless,' she told the nurse standing beside them. 'If it's just the flu then it's a nasty one, and I don't want anyone else catching it. And we'll get his temp down as soon as possible. I want cool, wet towels and a lumbar puncture tray—including a manometer.' She looked up, but before she voiced her next request Struan had placed an ophthalmoscope in her hand—anticipating her need. She flashed him a grateful glance and turned back to Jack.

The nurse was already moving, and Gina was relieved to see that she seemed efficient. If they didn't get that temperature down they ran the risk of Jack convulsing.

'How much penicillin did you give him?' she asked Struan as she bent to check the fundus—the back of Jack's eyes—to exclude the possibility of raised intra-cranial pressure. The consequences of doing a lumbar puncture when such pressure existed could be disastrous.

'Half a million units.'

She nodded. It should give them time. . . There didn't seem to be pressure.

'Take his temp again while I scrub,' Gina ordered, and Struan also moved fast to her command. Surprisingly, she thought. She would have expected the autocratic Struan Maitland to be jealous of his ascendancy. In medicine, though, you worked according to speciality. If she'd had an adult with a heart attack she'd do what Struan ordered. Now. . . Now, she was the paediatrician, and Struan was prepared to follow orders.

She scrubbed carefully, conscious of the fact that she'd been with the pup. The nurse had anticipated her needs and stood waiting with a sterile gown.

Struan and Jack's mum had already removed his clothes. The child didn't raise a protest as they wiped his hot little body with the cool towels.

'You're too hot,' Gina told the little boy as she returned. 'That's why you're feeling so bad. The wet towels will make you feel better. . .'

He didn't make any response as he lay limply in his mother's arms. Strange adults stripping him of his clothes and placing him on wet towelling. . . A well child would have been frantic with rage. Not Jack. . .

'Forty point six,' Struan said into her ear, and Gina winced. The temperature was going up. . .

'He's shivering,' the mother faltered. 'He's cold.'

'He has to be cold,' Gina told her. 'We must get this temperature down.'

'But it seems cruel. . .'

Not half as cruel as what was coming next, Gina thought grimly. She caught Struan's eye and he gave a sympathetic grimace. He was thinking the same.

They had to do it, though. To miss meningitis. . .

'Place him in position, will you, Dr Maitland?' Gina ordered, wondering which job she hated most—holding a child having this procedure, or performing the actual lumbar puncture. There was no doubt that she should do the puncture, though. The kindest way to do it was to do it fast, and only experience had made her fast. With years of training at one of the country's leading children's hospitals, she'd become as fast as she ever would be.

Struan manoeuvred the limp child into foetal position. A well child should have been fighting every inch of the way, here, and Gina had performed the test on children who were well.

Struan was carefully, skilfully, placing Jack on his side, his face away from them and his body with maximum bend of the spine, while Gina donned sterile gloves. To perform a lumbar puncture in anything less than aseptic conditions was a recipe for disaster. Behind them, the parents clutched each other for comfort. Finally, satisfied she was sterile, Gina swabbed the bare skin with antiseptic and carefully palpated the area at the third intervertebral space, searching for the right position. Then she glanced up at the parents.

'We're just taking a little fluid from his spinal column,' Gina told his parents gently. 'It won't take more than a couple of minutes—but would you like to wait outside?'

It seemed they would, the burly farmer urgently leading his wife out. His face was deathly white. Any longer, Gina thought, and she would have had more than one patient.

Turned to the wall, Jack didn't even realise his parents had left him. His eyes were dull with pain. Struan held him hard in position; Gina took a deep breath, prayed that she could be fast, and held out her hand for the needle. The nurse placed it into her gloved hand.

First time lucky. Gina felt her breath go out in a little rush of relief as the needle gently, carefully slid home, and she felt the almost imperceptible pop, or give, as it reached its right position. No matter how good the paediatrician, there were always times when the needle had to be inserted two or even three times before locating the correct place to draw off the fluid.

Jack didn't scream. He should have, Gina thought grimly. It would have made Struan's job tougher, but she had always found the less resistance there was, the sicker the child seemed to be.

She pulled the central needle out, leaving the outer needle in place. The cerebrospinal fluid oozed out in fast drops, and Gina grimaced as she noted that it was cloudy. Normal spinal fluid was clear.

She filled three small specimen containers with about one millilitre of the fluid and then the nurse handed her the manometer. Swiftly she attached it, almost hoping that Jack would start to fight. The pressure the manometer showed made her grimace further.

Not good. She glanced up at Struan and saw by his face that he knew the results as well as she did. It hardly needed pathology to confirm this. Then she lifted the needle clear, swabbed again with antiseptic, and the nurse moved in to cover the tiny needle-hole with a sterile dressing.

'That's that,' Gina said quietly, looking down at the syringe. She glanced up at the nurse. 'Bring his mum and dad back in before we turn him over.'

His mother came, but not his father. Mr Messer was in all sorts of trouble in the waiting-room conveniences. The woman was made of sterner stuff. Well, maybe not. She came in, gathered her little boy close and burst into tears.

'Can I dress him now?'

'He's better off with nothing on,' Struan told her, signalling Gina with his eyes to take her containers and go. The sooner she knew what she was holding in her hand, the better.

Bacterial meningitis. . .

Gina stared down through the microscope and swore. She'd rung Tony, the lab technician, to come in, but before he arrived she'd performed the initial microscopy herself. It didn't need a lab technician to tell her what the problem was. There were obvious bacteria in the spinal fluid.

'Damn. . .' She looked up as Tony came in. 'Check this, will you, Tony?'

Tony looked, and swore as well.

'I'm right, aren't I?' Gina asked.

'Yep. Bacterial meningitis. Whose is the fluid?'

'Jack Messer.'

'Whew. . .' Tony whistled. 'Poor little blighter. He's only tiny. . .'

'It's bad whatever age,' Gina said. 'Do a protein and glucose level for me, Tony, and then put it up for culture. I'm going back to the ward.'

By the time she returned, Jack had been moved into the children's ward. With Lisa gone he was the only occupant, and Gina silently blessed herself for taking Lisa away. The last thing the little girl needed was the makings of another tragedy.

Struan met her at the door. 'Meningitis?'

'Yes. And it's bacterial.' There were two forms of meningitis—viral, which was usually a much less aggressive disease, and the bacterial form Jack was suffering from.

'OK.' Struan was on clear ground now. 'Let's get some intravenous fluid and antibiotic started now. Sister,' he called, 'I want a stand set up immediately. How much antibiotic, Gina?'

Gina looked down at the bed. If Jack had been well at lunch-time the disease was moving fast. . .

'Let's hit him hard,' she said, and named a dose that made Struan's eyebrows raise. 'If we don't, we risk losing him,' she said in an undertone that only Struan could hear. Her lips tightened. 'I guess you know we risk losing him anyway.'

She stayed with the little boy until after midnight. The child was almost unconscious, drifting in and out of delirium. His mother stayed as well, haggard and hopeless, unable to believe how quickly catastrophe had overtaken them.

Gina checked the drips and washed and washed the burning little body, willing the temperature to drop just a fraction.

'Come on, Jack,' she murmured, over and over again. 'You can fight this thing.'

Struan was elsewhere in the hospital, looking after his stroke patient. There was nothing more he could do for Jack and it would have just added unnecessary fear to the parents to have two doctors present.

Gina went over and over the treatment in her head, but there was nothing more she could do. It was so darned hard—to sit and wait.

'Can't we send him to Melbourne?' the mother asked at one stage. Her husband had been forced to go home to care for the other children, and she was rigid with strain.

'There's nothing more they could do there,' Gina assured her. 'I promise you that, Mrs Messer. And the strain of the trip might well be enough to tip Jack over the edge. We just hold on here.'

Hold on. . .

It was all she was doing. With the antibiotics up and the fluid running she had done all she could. At least the child wasn't vomiting. His fluid levels must be rising again.

At about two, Struan returned. He looked as exhausted as Gina felt.

Penny Messer was asleep, her head resting on her son's bed. Gina felt like doing the same, but she wasn't taking her eyes from the child for a moment. If they'd had a trained ICU sister available to special. . .

They didn't. With the dramas unfolding elsewhere in the hospital she was on her own, except for one single certificate nurse. And if Jack convulsed then she needed to be there, right then.

'Hey. . .' Struan's hand came down on her shoulder

and she jumped. She hadn't heard him approach. 'How goes it?'

Gina sighed. 'No change.'

'No convulsions?'

'No.'

'Well, that's a good sign in itself.'

'And your lady?'

'She died ten minutes ago.'

'I'm sorry.'

'Don't be,' Struan told her. 'Edna was ninety-four and she's been well until tonight. The stroke would have left her permanently impaired. Until yesterday she was one of our gardeners, and now she's gone. She wouldn't have wanted it any other way.'

Gina nodded and looked down at the little boy. It was a far different story from Jack.

A nurse walked in behind them and Struan looked up and smiled. 'Rhonda,' he said gratefully. 'Gina, Rhonda—Sister Rhodes—has been helping me until now, but she can take over here. She's ICU-trained. What's more, Rhonda is on night duty, so she gets to sleep tomorrow. Which is more than we will.'

Gina looked dubiously at the little boy and then up to Rhonda's capable face. 'You'll call me if there's any change?'

'I certainly will,' Rhonda promised.

'So bed, Dr Buchanan,' Struan ordered. 'Now.'

He escorted her firmly over to the door of the children's ward and then down the corridor to the door of her flat. In the dim light of her living-room Lisa and Wacky slept on, Sam Tiger wedged precariously between them.

'That's quite a family you have there, Dr Buchanan,' Struan said drily as he lifted the barrier to let her through. She'd shoved a trolley on its side against the door, to stop Wacky escaping. 'Especially for someone who doesn't want one.'

'I never said I didn't want one.'

'No.' He rubbed his hand wearily through his black hair. 'You want a family on your terms—a family without the capacity to hurt you.' He looked across at Lisa and Wacky. 'Well, maybe you have that there, but have you thought about your capacity to hurt them?'

'What. . .what do you mean?'

'I mean that Lisa's already reacting disastrously to your leaving. The nurses told me just how upset she's been. Is it fair to Lisa to strengthen ties you can't maintain?'

Gina fell silent. Criticism—and justified criticism.

'What. . .? What would you have me do?' she asked.

'Leave her in the kids' ward.'

Gina's eyes flew up to his. 'You'd do that?'

'If you don't have any intention of a long-term relationship then it might be kinder to make her develop the armour she has to have. By protecting her—well, she'll stay vulnerable to pain for so much longer.'

'Armour doesn't stop the pain.'

'No.' He looked at her. 'You'd know that, wouldn't you, Gina? But it can stop the wounds being crippling. It can make you able to feel pain, but still capable of facing the world while you ache. Like you do.'

He knew. He could see so far inside her that there was no corner unexposed. Where was her armour now?

'We'll have to organise foster-care,' Struan was saying. 'Fast.'

'But. . .'

'What if we go out tomorrow night and face Sandra? If she still insists she doesn't want anything to do with the child then we can see if she knows where Lisa's father is. Get things rolling before Social Welfare become involved. Then, if we're lucky, she might qualify for long-term fostering. Or even adoption.'

Why did Gina's heart feel leaden at the thought?

She looked across at the sleeping child clutching her beloved puppy, and she wanted to weep.

'OK,' she said dully. 'We'll go and see Sandra.'

'Fine.' He smiled down at her and his hand moved to cup her chin. He forced her eyes up to his.

'You know, for someone who's made a vow not to expose themselves to pain, you're making a pretty fair fist of doing just that, Gina Buchanan. That heart of yours isn't capable of doing anything else.'

He stood looking down at her for a long, long moment, and then gently stooped to kiss her on the lips.

'Goodnight, then, my love,' he said softly. 'You need your sleep. Put yourself to bed, fast, but keep me in your dreams.'

CHAPTER TEN

To HER fury she did just that. Gina tossed and turned during a troubled night's sleep, with images of Struan and Lisa, and Wacky and little Jack all intertwined. Trouble seemed all around her, but enmeshing all were Struan's caring eyes.

'Goodnight, my love. . .'

It was a whisper of blessing all around her, seductive in its promise.

She wanted to give in to him so badly. It would be so easy to place his magnificent diamond on her finger and abandon herself to the promise in his eyes.

But with that promise. . .

With that promise lay the demand for commitment—the demand that she open herself wholly to him.

And trust him.

Trust. . . That was the rub, wasn't it? To trust that he wouldn't hurt her. . .wouldn't leave her. . . Wouldn't come off his damned motorbike some stormy night and leave her bereft and wide open to the pain she'd so carefully learned to shield herself from.

She couldn't bear it. No. . . If it meant she stayed single for the rest of her life, then so be it. She had hoped she could be happy with Wayne. Well, some things were impossible. Family without commitment. . .

So. . . So her family was Wacky.

And Lisa. . .?

Lisa? Of all the crazy ideas. . . She sat straight up in bed and swore. What was she doing? How unprofessional was this—to be considering long-term commitment to a patient?

'And Lisa's still just a patient, Gina Buchanan,' she said aloud harshly. A child who needed her professional assistance before she got on with her life, but who had to go on without her. 'So don't you forget it. You go out to see Sandra tomorrow and get foster-care arrangements under way. And you act like the professional paediatrician you are, instead of a mushy teenager.

'But that's how I feel,' she whispered into her pillow as she drifted again into troubled sleep. 'In fact I don't even feel that old.'

She was woken before her alarm went off by two bodies landing simultaneously on her bed. One child. One pup.

'Wacky's done a puddle on his newspaper,' Lisa announced excitedly. 'Isn't he clever, Dr Buchanan?'

'Practically Einstein.' Gina rubbed bleary eyes and looked at the clock. Six-thirty. . . Four hours of sleep.

'He's done another one on the kitchen lino,' Lisa confessed. 'But that was first and I growled at him, so then he did another one on the newspaper.'

'His training's almost completed, then. Only jumping through burning hoops to go.'

Lisa eyed her suspiciously. 'I don't think he should learn burning hoops. He might burn himself. What's for breakfast?'

Child and pup bounced simultaneously and looked at Gina with such eager eyes that Gina burst out laughing. Was this the same apathetic child she had come home to yesterday?

'Go away, you horrible pair,' she told them with mock-severity. 'Go and teach Wacky to do puddles on the lawn. I'm going to have a shower before anyone has breakfast.'

'We had a banana from the fruit bowl,' Lisa told her. 'I ate mine.'

'We. . .' Gina looked at Wacky. '*We* had a banana? You and Wacky, both?'

'Wacky spat his out,' Lisa confessed. 'I was going to clean it up but I didn't know where the mop was.'

Gina burst out laughing. Visions of mopped banana filled her imagination and she thanked her stars the mop was concealed. It seemed there were domestic chores waiting.

'I'd better start, then, or I'll be late for work.'

Lisa's face fell. 'You're going to work?'

'Only here.' Gina gave her a hard, reassuring hug. 'I'll pop in whenever I can, and one of the nurses will be watching you through the door, but one of the reasons I brought you here is so you can look after Wacky. I can't leave him alone, now, can I?'

'No.' Lisa looked important. 'So I'm babysitting?'

'You certainly are. Starting now. Off you go, you babysitter extraordinaire, and babysit your charge. Outside until I'm dressed.'

As soon as child and pup disappeared, Gina picked up the extension phone and dialled the children's ward. Rhonda answered on the second ring.

'You haven't called,' Gina started. She held her breath. Surely Rhonda wouldn't have ignored instructions?

'I haven't needed to. There's been no change.'

'Temp?'

'Still on thirty-nine eight.'

'OK. I'll be with you soon.'

There was too much to worry about, Gina thought grimly as she showered and prepared breakfast for three. Too much for one woman to contend with.

Maybe not. Gina stood by Jack's bed and looked down at him, her fingers holding the thin little wrist as she took his pulse. Maybe the pulse was a little stronger. . .?

She wasn't imagining it. The child was still hot with fever, but his colour was slightly better. As she held his wrist the little one stirred, opened his eyes and looked up fearfully.

'I want my mummy. . .'

It was a thread of a cry, but it was a cry for all that.

'Your mum's fast asleep,' Gina told him. She glanced up to see Struan swing into the ward, white-coated and efficient. She blocked his presence out. 'Look.' She pointed to the next bed, where Mrs Messer was sleeping.

The child was too weak to argue further. He twisted slightly so that he was facing his mother and then his eyes closed again.

'There's been no vomiting or diarrhoea?' Gina asked.

'None.'

'Urine output?'

'Two wet beds, neither very large.'

'Then he must be building up his fluid content again.' Gina breathed out slowly. 'Maybe. . .I think we're looking like we have a good chance here.'

'Surely it's too early?' Rhonda stared.

'Too early to be sure,' Gina agreed. 'But he's definitely improved from last night, and if meningitis kills, it usually doesn't show any signs of relenting on the way.' She closed her eyes for a second, remembering a child she had helped treat as a registrar. He'd eaten his tea happily and had been dead by midnight.

It wasn't going to happen to Jack. Not this time. . .

'We might be on a winner, Dr Buchanan.' Struan had come up behind her and laid a hand lightly on her shoulder. 'It's still early, but so far. . . Well done.'

'You gave the initial penicillin,' Gina told him. 'If you'd waited. . .'

'But I'm not much of a hand at waiting,' he said softly. 'I find it's a dangerous course.' His eyes met hers and there was a very definite message there. Unmistakable.

'I. . . Call me when Mrs Messer wakes,' Gina said helplessly to Rhonda, trying to drag her eyes from Struan. 'I believe. . .I believe there's work I should be doing.'

'Your first day of rostered duty.' Struan's eyes were still caressing, and Gina could feel her face burning under Rhonda's interested gaze. 'I'm here to show you what's expected.'

Gina took a deep breath. 'Fine,' she said tightly. 'Show me.'

There was nothing she couldn't handle. Routine checks of nursing home patients, arthritis clinic—which she'd have to brush up on as her contact with osteoarthritis as a paediatrician was limited—emergency casualty admitting officer—'And we had enough emergencies last night, so I'll thank you to discourage any more,' Struan told her—and on-call duty for the local doctors until they could reach the hospital in the case of a drama with their patients.

'You should be fine,' Struan told her. 'The job occupies Lloyd full-time because he's young and unsure, but you should even have time to housetrain that pup.'

Personally, Gina doubted it, but in the end he was proved right. She was an experienced doctor, with a learned instinct for differentiating between minor and major ailments. She wasn't used to elderly patients, but found the work very familiar, and she wasn't so far divorced from her general training to be at a disadvantage.

And it was good to be busy. Good to feel needed.

She was needed in more ways than one. Struan had told her she wouldn't be fully occupied, but she had constant visits to Jack in the children's ward, and what spare time remained was more than occupied by the pair back in her flat. The children's ward staff treated Lisa as a patient, lifing her over the dividing wall to give her a bath and find her games, but Lisa was determined to stay on Gina's side of the door as much as she could. She brightened every time Gina returned, and by the end of the day Gina was wondering just what she'd let herself in for.

'You'll have tea with the children's ward staff,' Gina told Lisa as she gave Wacky his meaty bites. 'I have to make a house-call.'

It must only be referred to as a house-call as far as Lisa was concerned. She couldn't tell Lisa that the call was to plead with Sandra for Lisa's future.

Lisa's face fell. 'I'd rather have tea with you.'

'I know.' Gina gave her a swift hug. 'But I'm a doctor, Lisa, and you're staying in a working girl's flat. You have the choice to go back to hospital if you're lonely.'

'I'm staying here,' Lisa said solidly. She cast a scared glance up at Gina. 'Forever, if you'll let me.'

Forever. . . Gina's heart sank. What had she done? Stuck an unprofessional oar in? Made matters worse?

She couldn't let herself see into Lisa's future. More and more, the fate of the little girl was part of an agonised knot of pain twisted with Gina's own past.

She went back to the children's ward before she left—to check on Jack Messer yet again. She'd been in the ward every twenty minutes during the day, checking fluid levels and hoping.

Mr and Mrs Messer were by their child's bedside, their haggard faces a matched set. Gina's heart went out to them. To sit and wait was the hardest part.

She picked up the chart and stared. The last temperature reading was thirty-eight nine. It was the first time it had dropped below thirty-nine. She looked at her watch. This had been taken almost half an hour ago.

'Can you repeat the temperature reading now?' she asked the nurse. A young, sharp-faced nurse with pencil-lined eyebrows and too much lipstick was laconically surveying the group around the bed.

'It's not due for five minutes.'

'I want it done now, please, Nurse.' Gina sighed, mentally deciding to talk to the girl later. Rigid adherence to instructions was all very well, but to question a doctor's instructions on such a trivial thing. . .

The girl gave an almost perceptible flounce as she crossed to the bed and lifted the thermometer from its holder, but as she started to poke it towards Jack, Gina stopped her. She held the girl's hand back and took the thermometer from her, reading her name-tag as she did.

'Not in anger, please, Suzanne,' she said gently. She glanced at her watch and frowned, realising the probable cause of the girl's annoyance. 'Are you almost due for shift-change?'

'Yes,' the belligerent Suzanne retorted. 'And the next obs are the responsibility of the next shift.'

Whew. . .

'No doubt you have an important date that makes taking an extra temperature a nuisance?' Gina's voice was soft, her mounting anger carefully controlled. Medical staff who'd worked with Gina in the past would have recognised her tone and grown wary— very wary. As it was, the girl flounced a little more and grew still more aggressive. Gina might be a doctor but she was young and female, and she had less make-up on. . .

'I have, as a matter of fact,' Suzanne said belligerently. She stared at Gina with wide, mocking eyes. 'With Wayne Macky. . . He says he's not engaged to you any more.'

'Well, bully for you,' Gina said softly. She turned away from the girl, trying to hide the relief on her face. So Wayne wasn't wasting time. That was one load off her conscience.

'Off you go, then, Suzanne,' she told the nurse, without looking up. 'I'll do your obs for you. Have a lovely time.' Then, because she couldn't resist, she threw another question. 'Is he taking you to the Steak Supreme?'

'Yes, he is.' Belligerence was still there, but Gina's unexpected response had stirred a touch of anxiety.

Gina nodded. 'Have fun. And, Nurse?'

'Yes?'

'Be in my office at nine tomorrow morning. I wish to have a word with you.'

The girl stared. She flushed a delicate shade of pink and looked uncertainly at the thermometer. 'Do you want me to take the temperature, then?'

'I want you to go,' Gina told her. 'Your place is not here.'

She turned back to her little patient, lifted his arm and slid the glass tube against his skin. Matter closed. Until tomorrow. . .

'Struth. . .' The father gave a short, worried laugh. 'I'm glad I'm not in her shoes.'

'She's young,' Gina smiled absently, feeling Jack's pulse.

'She's not coming back to the children's ward.' It was Struan, standing by the door. How long had he been there? He strode across to the bed and looked from one anxious parent to the other. 'You needn't worry. If she approaches your son like that we'll find someone else to take her place. An attitude like that to patient-care is unforgivable in any hospital I run.' He looked at Gina. 'How goes it?'

'We'll see in a moment.' Gina looked down at the sleeping child. 'But he seems in a more natural sleep.'

Struan nodded and waited. Three long minutes. . .
It took longer to take an under-arm temperature, but
it was dangerous to put a thermometer in the mouth
of a child this sick. If he suddenly convulsed. . .

He didn't. Jack slept soundly on, and finally Gina
pulled the thermometer out. The tiny glass panel confirmed what the feel of Jack's forehead under her hand
had suggested.

'Thirty-eight two,' Gina smiled. She looked up at
the parents and held the thermometer for them to
confirm for themselves what she was telling them. 'I
think. . .I think we might be out of the woods.'

'Really?' The woman looked at Gina as though Gina
might be perpetrating some cruel joke, and Gina
leaned across the bed to take her hand.

'Really. He's still a sick little boy, and if I were you
I'd stay here again tonight with him, but it's my bet
he'll be well enough to take some fluids tomorrow—
all by himself.'

Struan was feeling Jack's pulse and he nodded.
'There's no doubt,' he told the parents. He smiled
down at the little boy. 'It seems your Jack is fighting
back, and it's my bet that from here on, he's going
to win.'

They left Jack's parents to their bedside vigil, their
tense faces slightly relaxed but still watchful. Rhonda
was in charge for the night so they could leave him in
good hands.

'And Lesley's in the labour-room with yet another
mid,' Struan told Gina. 'And it's straightforward, so
she's free if Rhonda needs her. We can go without
being missed.'

Except by Lisa. . . Except by Wacky. . . For
heaven's sake, where was Gina's independent
existence now?

She sat silently by Struan on the short drive to
Sandra's home, trying to come to terms with what was

happening to her. She was leaving this place as soon as Lloyd returned. She was. So. . .

So she had to persuade Sandra to take Lisa—or organise good foster-care. She couldn't be responsible for the child's long-term care.

Could she?

She looked sideways at Struan's lean, thoughtful face. He seemed intent on the road, content to leave her with her own problems. It was almost as though he was playing a waiting-game—waiting until she was ready to fall into his arms.

She gave herself an angry mental shake. She'd slept with him, hadn't she? What more did he want of her?

He wants to marry you. The words whispered over and over in her mind, like a hypnotic dream. Give in to his lure. . .

'Well, well. . .' Struan looked out at the lighted street at a couple walking hand in hand into a familiar building. The Steak Supreme. 'That's a fast replacement job.'

Suzanne and Wayne. . . Gina bit her lip, a faint flush of mortification rising at Wayne's fast desertion of intentions. OK, she'd called it off, but he could have acted a little more hurt.

'Will we sack the pair of them?' Struan asked idly, and Gina stared.

'Don't. . . Don't be absurd.'

'They've got to go,' he told her. 'But maybe we should wait. I'll tell Macky tomorrow that he should start looking for a replacement position.'

'There's no need to do that because——' Gina struggled for words. 'For me. I mean, he should be allowed to stay.'

'No.' Struan shook his head. 'I'd had Wayne Macky up to the eyebrows when you arrived on the scene. Because of you I thought I might have to put up with the creep. Now. . . Now he can go, and take his new girlfriend with him.'

Gina stared. 'You mean. . . You mean, you weren't going to sack Wayne because of me?'

He glanced over at her. 'Yes.' He smiled. 'Because you're a damned good doctor and you intended marrying Wayne, all of us—the medical partners in the town—decided we'd put up with Wayne a bit longer. But not now.'

'That's. . .that's quite a compliment.'

'It's meant to be. You're a fine doctor, Gina Buchanan.'

'You know. . . You know I'm leaving anyway? As soon as Lloyd gets back.'

He raised his eyebrows. 'Are you, indeed?'

'I'm not. . .I can't keep working here.'

'Because of Wayne?'

'Because of you.'

He nodded. 'I see,' he said, in a voice that said he didn't see at all. He pulled the car off the road. 'Well, that's all very interesting, Dr Buchanan, but for now. . . For now we have one reluctant aunt to deal with. Let's get one problem out of the way before we face another, shall we?'

Reluctant?

Sandra wasn't reluctant. She was angry and aggressive and defiant. She opened the door to them and her attitude met them like a physical blow.

'I'm not having the kid,' she said savagely. 'I know that's what you've come about. Jenny tricked me into saying I'd look after the kid. She knew she was going to knock herself off. I'm damned if I'll be tricked into taking on responsibilities she didn't have the guts to bear.'

'Sandra, can we speak to you for a moment?' Struan's hands went out to grasp Sandra's, deflecting her aggression with touch. 'I know you're angry. I would be too, if I thought Jenny had tricked you. But she didn't, Sandra.'

'She committed suicide. She had a choice.'

'She had terminal cancer.'

'Cancer. . .? You're kidding. . .'

'No, Sandra. We're not.'

Sandra withdrew her hands from Struan's, the anger fading from her eyes. 'You'd better. . . You'd better come in,' she managed.

What followed was a difficult hour. Sandra sat listlessly at the kitchen table, trying hard to come to terms with what she was hearing.

'Why. . .? Why didn't she tell me?'

In the end anger rose again. It was almost as though concealing the cancer was as big a betrayal as the suicide.

Finally Sandra's husband came home—a big man with his propensity for heavy drinking already showing on his face. He stood at the door and listened all over again to what Struan had to say, and Sandra's anger was reflected in his eyes.

'It's not going to make a bit of bloody difference,' he snapped, casting an aggressive glance at his wife. 'I'm not having another kid for any bloody reason. And that's that.'

Sandra bit her lip. It seemed Jenny's cancer had softened her a little—but not much.

'We can't keep her.' She spread her hands on the table. 'You can see that, can't you?' she pleaded with the two doctors.

'Yes,' Struan agreed. In the face of this anger and dislike, to push Lisa into this household would be to court disaster. 'I can see that.'

'But. . .' Sandra's eyes filled with helpless tears. 'I did promise Jenny. I suppose. . .I mean, if we can find someone local who'd have her. . .I could still see her then. Pop in sometimes. . . Just to make sure she was all right, like. . .'

'That'd be the best solution,' Struan said, his eyes flicking to Gina. 'But. . .'

'But?'

'But there aren't a lot of foster-care families in Gundowring. It might be different if we could arrange adoption. There are more families looking for a child they can consider their own.'

Sandra's lips tightened. 'It won't. . . We can't have her adopted.'

'Why not?'

'Well. . .' she glanced at her husband. 'We might. . . Later on, I mean. . .'

Gina's heart sank. This was the nightmare that the Social Welfare department loathed. Relatives who wouldn't take responsibility but who wouldn't relinquish their hold. And who wanted the right just to 'pop in'. It was good for the child to maintain contact, but it often ended as an impossible situation for the foster-family—and prospective foster-families knew it.

'Lisa's father——?' she started.

'We don't know where he is,' Sandra told her. 'He was an American, over here doing some sort of computer contract work. He lit out when Jenny became pregnant—confessed he had a wife and children back home—and hasn't been seen since.'

Terrific. Gina found her fingers clenched into fists on the Laminex table. What sort of future was there for the child under these conditions?

'So you won't agree to adoption?'

'Well, she can't be adopted, can she?' Sandra demanded, a trifle smugly. 'Not if her dad can't be found, and I can't even remember his name. And no— I wouldn't agree to it. What do you reckon, Trev?'

Her husband, when appealed to, seemed to have no opinion at all. 'As long as I don't have anything to do with her I couldn't give a stuff,' he growled.

Struan rose. There was no point going on. They were doing no good at all.

'Will you still visit her?' Struan asked. 'The Social Welfare people will come on Friday but she'll be at the hospital until then.' He flicked another glance at Gina, but obviously decided against telling them of Gina's arrangement to have Lisa in her flat.

'I reckon I won't for a while, if it's all the same to you,' Sandra said stiffly. 'I. . . It'd upset me to see her. . .I mean, after hearing about Jenny and that. . .'

'It'd upset her. . .' As soon as they were safely back in the car, Gina exploded. 'It'd upset Sandra! Not one word about how upset Lisa will be to lose aunt and cousins as well as her mother. And she's just destroyed any chance Lisa might have of finding a family long-term.'

'You don't know that.'

'I can make a darned good guess.'

'So it's up to us to ensure she finds good foster-care.'

'And how are we to do that? You know she won't be kept here. The bulk of foster-families are in the city—and you also know foster-families are usually unhappy about having a child where they're likely to be inundated with interfering relatives. Would you have a short-term foster-child in this town?'

'I might,' Struan said diffidently. 'If it meant so much to you.'

Gina stared across at him in the darkness. 'What's. . .? What's that supposed to mean?'

Struan didn't answer. Instead he pulled the car off the main road on to a rough track leading up to the headland. He didn't speak again until the car was parked facing out to the mooonlit sea. Then he turned to her.

'I still have an engagement ring in my pocket,' he

said softly. 'And they'd let us foster Lisa.'

Gina's world spun on some tilted axis. She put her hand to her head, as though it hurt. 'You're. . . You're asking me to marry you to give Lisa a home?'

'I'm asking you to marry me because I love you.' He didn't move to touch her but his eyes held her all the same, dark and compelling in the moon's silver sheen. 'And I'm not offering to take on Lisa without thinking about it. I think. . .I think we could be a family, Gina. But it's up to you.'

The world still spun. To her horror Gina felt her eyes fill with tears. Damn this man. He could sit here and look at her like this and she'd turn to jelly—she'd melt into tears, and she despised tears. She hadn't cried since. . .

No.

That was what she was trying so hard to avoid. A man who could make her cry. . .

'You can't bribe me into marrying you,' she whispered.

'I'm offering, Gina. I'm not bribing.' Still he didn't touch her. No pressure, his eyes told her. Just understanding and love and. . .

And damned tears! Gina wiped her face angrily with the back of her hand. 'Struan, I'm not marrying you. I know. . . Look, I know it'd be good for Lisa, but maybe. . .just maybe I can look after Lisa on my own.'

'You mean, give her security but not risk your precious emotional independence?'

'Struan. . .' She put her hands out pleadingly, and then let tham fall back. 'You have to understand. If I let myself love you. . .'

'You already do.'

She ignored that. 'If I let myself love you. . . If I married you and then anything happened—if. . .I mean, even if you died. . .I don't think. . .I couldn't cope, Struan.'

'So your answer to that is not to marry. Not to let yourself love.' In his voice there was the beginning of anger.

'Of course it is,' she said helplessly. 'It has to be. Struan, I'm not capable of losing any more. . .'

'Then you can't win either.'

'That's right. So I'm not joining the race. I'm standing on the sidelines, Struan. I made that decision years ago and I'm darned if your emotional blackmail is going to upset my decision.' She closed her eyes. 'It can't. I. . .I daren't.'

'So I get to stand on the sidelines too, because you lack courage?'

Gina took a deep breath. 'That's the way it has to be, Struan. I'm. . . Please. . .I'm sorry. But I just can't. . .'

'You just can't fall in love?'

'I already have,' Gina admitted helplessly, and then put her hands out to fend him off. 'But I have to fall out of love just as fast. Because I can't. . .I can't bear it. I can't bear the agony of waiting for it to end.'

'So you'll end it before it begins?'

'That's right,' she whispered. 'That's the way it has to be.'

CHAPTER ELEVEN

IT WAS just as well the next days were busy. If Gina hadn't been flat out with her hospital work and care of Lisa and the dog, she might have gone quietly crazy. A tight knot of grief was permanently wrapped around her heart.

'It has to be like this,' she whispered to herself over and over again. 'OK, it hurts to tell Struan you don't want him. But this way—this way you get the hurt over now.'

A faded photograph of her father lay at the bottom of her suitcase. She took it out and Struan's eyes laughed out of the frame at her. There was also a photograph of her mother, taken the year after he'd left them. Those two pictures, side by side, were enough to make her know she was right.

So. . .

So she talked with Struan when she had no choice, but at other times she avoided him. When he approached her she was civil, and that was all. She could see anger and frustration building, but there was nothing she could do about that. She had enough of her own demons to worry about before she could concern herself with Struan's.

'Anyone who falls in love in days can fall out of love just as fast,' she told herself savagely, but she didn't believe it for a moment. Not when the rule was being applied to her.

Busy. . . She had to keep busy. It was the only way to keep her sanity.

On Wednesday night she finished early, and on impulse took Lisa and Wacky to the beach for tea. It wasn't as happy a meal as she'd hoped—echoes of the last time she'd eaten on the beach with Lisa were too vivid—but child and pup rolled in the sand, and for a small time Lisa seemed a carefree little girl again.

Friday. . .

That was looming closer too. Gina had looked bitterly at the options available and had known it was pure fantasy to think she could care for Lisa herself. She'd borrowed heavily to put herself through medical school and some of the debt was still outstanding. There wasn't money for permanent child-care—and her hours were long. It wasn't fair on Lisa even to think of it.

So Lisa would be taken into foster-care. Friday. . .

She looked at the little girl splashing in the shallows and knew that Friday couldn't be the end of her relationship with Lisa. She could still visit her.

Like Wayne.

The thought was immeasurably bleak. She'd only had Wayne, and Lisa would end up seeing Gina with the same sense of gratitude. It was only now that Gina realised that gratitude was a burden in itself.

Damn. . . She had come to the beach to be happy and she was growing more maudlin by the moment. Slowly she packed away the picnic things and called to Lisa. As she did a figure up in the sand-dunes caught her eye.

The beach was deserted. Seven at night— Gundowring residents were home having tea, seated at their kitchen tables like civilised human beings. There was only Gina, Lisa and Wacky on the beach.

And someone was watching them. A man. . . He was silhouetted against the setting sun, only a shape in the distance, but something about him made Gina sharpen her voice to Lisa.

'Come on, you pair. Let's go home.'

'Oh, Gina. . .' Lisa's use of the formal 'Dr Buchanan' had faded fast.

'Quickly!' Her voice was sharper than she'd intended and Lisa and pup responded, looking up at her curiously as she hurried them up the beach.

'Why do we have to go?'

'Because. . . Because Wacky's tired.' The pup was racing in tight circles around their feet, making a liar of her, and Gina bit her lip. She was being stupid—jumping at shadows. She looked up at the sand-hills again and the man had gone. Stupid. . .

'You're going too fast,' Lisa complained. 'My legs aren't as long as yours.'

'No,' Gina smiled, slowing her pace and taking Lisa by the hand. 'They're not, are they, Lisa, love? We'll go home slowly.'

Would she spend the rest of her life living in fear? Gina went to bed early and lay watching the moonlight cast silver threads over her ceiling. She was so darned nervous. The man on the beach had been no threat—probably a local taking a stroll along the beach before he went home for dinner—and her reaction had been silly.

You've been scared since you were a child, she accused herself. Will you stay scared forever?

'I'm not scared for me,' She told the moonlight. It was true. She wasn't. She was frightened for those she loved.

And she loved Lisa—and Wacky—and Struan. . .

'Oh, for heaven's sake. . . Shut up and get on with your life.' She turned over and buried her head in the pillow, and then swore as the telephone beside the bed rang.

She wasn't on call tonight. Her patients—even little Jack—were all looking good.

Still. . . It was only nine-thirty. Hardly an uncivilised

time to call. She put a hand out from the bedclothes and lifted the receiver.

'Gina?'

'Lloyd?' Gina recognised the voice and sat bolt-upright in bed, her annoyance forgotten. 'Lloyd, how lovely to hear from you.'

'Yeah. . .' She could hear pleasure in his voice through the line. Pleasure. . .

'Something's happened?'

'It sure has.' He paused, savouring the moment. 'I'm wriggling both sets of toes.'

'You're——'

'I thought I could move my left ones a little at the weekend—but so little I thought I was imagining it. Today they moved so much that the doctors could see the movement—and the feeling's coming back into the right foot.'

'Oh, Lloyd. . . That's fantastic.' For this much feeling to have returned so soon meant there was little likelihood of paraplegia—if any. As long as the traction stayed on until the break healed.

'Don't you do too much too soon,' she said anxiously, and Lloyd's answering grin was in his words.

'No, ma'am. I aim to be real careful. Model patient. I know the consequences of being anything else and it doesn't appeal.'

'Lloyd, that's great news.' Relief was flooding through Gina in waves. The thought of Lloyd's injuries and her responsibility for them had been almost unbearable.

'I thought you'd like to know.' He paused, and then said more gently, 'I guess I know what you've been going through.'

Another man who read her like a book? Gina sighed. Was she so transparent?

'Gina. . . There's something else.' The pleasure had faded and Gina frowned.

'Yes?'

'Look, I shouldn't tell you this. The police don't want to worry you, but I think you ought to know. Michael Carter—the guy who started all this—escaped from custody this morning.'

'Escaped?'

'He was being transferred from the remand centre and the van was involved in a minor collision. He took off and hasn't been seen since. Gina. . .'

'Yes?' Gina's mouth was dry.

'They've probably already caught him—but we'd be the last to know. I only know about the escape because it was on the news tonight, and all I have to do in this darned bed is watch TV. But I just thought. . . Well, you know what the man's capable of. Stick close to the hospital until he's caught.'

'I'll do that,' she promised.

'And tell Struan.'

'OK.'

He relaxed again and she could hear the smile come back into his voice. 'I hear it's all off with Wayne, then, Gina?'

'Who told you that?'

He lowered his voice mysteriously. 'I have sources. Gina. . .?'

'Yes?'

He hesitated, as though not sure whether or not to say something. Finally he continued. 'Gina, you and Struan. . .I gather. . . Well, Struan's been ringing me every night. I gather he has serious intentions in your direction.'

'*He* might have,' Gina said bitterly, and Lloyd laughed.

'Look, I don't know what's between the pair of you, but all I can say is that it's a real pleasure to have Struan with his smile back.'

'His smile back?' Gina lay back on her pillows and

stared at the ceiling. 'What? What do you mean?'

'Well, there hasn't been a lot of laughter for Struan since Sara died.' He grimaced into the phome and Gina could hear it in his voice. 'I don't know how much you've been told, but they'd been engaged for a month when Sara ran her car off the road and was killed. It happened nearly three years back, but Struan's been moving in a fog of pain since then—until you. You've brought the laughter back.'

'How. . .?' Gina could hardly trust her voice. 'How do you know this?'

'Everyone at Gundowring does,' Lloyd said simply. 'Sara was a local—a nurse. Hasn't anyone told you?'

'They have now.' Gina still stared silently upward, remembering a conversation in her head. Three proposals, Struan had said. And Gina hadn't even heard the pain behind his blank statement. 'And, yes, Lloyd, I guess someone did tell me,' she whispered. 'But I was too caught up in what was happening to me to listen.'

'That's understandable,' Lloyd sid consolingly. 'You've had a tough couple of weeks. How's the leg?'

'It's fine.' She was no longer listening, and had to jerk herself back to say the words. 'Look, Lloyd, I have to go. Thank you for ringing. It's terrific about your toes.'

'Yeah, it is, isn't it? And you be careful of Carter.'

'What? Oh, yes. Yes, Lloyd, I will. Goodnight.'

A dead fiancé. . .

Gina lay and let her mind drift over and over the thought of death in Struan's past.

She had been so caught up in her own pain—in her own emotional indecision—that she had never queried his. She had regarded Struan as light-hearted and dangerous, intent on marrying her out of hand without a thought to the future. She had thought he was unscarred—that he didn't know what it was to hurt.

And he had lost his laughter for three long years. He had lost his Sara.

'I've been selfish,' she whispered into the dark, and accepted it for the truth. She had looked no further than her own needs. She wasn't prepared to take a risk—and Struan was.

Struan knew what it was to lose—and yet he was prepared to take the chance. He was prepared to inflict pain on himself—in fact, maybe he already had. He had asked her to marry him and she had refused—because she wouldn't expose herself to the pain he had already suffered.

'It shouldn't make a difference,' she whispered. 'It shouldn't. . .'

It did, though. Of course it did.

Oh, Struan. . . Her body ached for him in her lonely bed and she twisted with the agony of indecision. It would be so easy to give in to him—forget the past and hope. . .

How could she forget the past? How was she to find courage to hope?

She might as well have stayed out of bed for all the sleep Gina had that night. She drifted off some time before dawn, but her dreams were dreadful, and when Lisa and Wacky launched their boisterous greeting she was almost grateful.

Thursday. . .

Today was Thursday. Tomorrow the Social Welfare people were coming from Melbourne—and Lisa would be taken away.

How to prepare the child for this? Gina's paediatric training was useless. She sat up in bed, reading a silly story from the children's ward library, and a feeling of helplessness threatened to engulf her.

Maybe she should tell Struan she'd marry him?

For Lisa? Ridiculous!

For you, her heart whispered, but she shook her head over child and dog. She mustn't listen to her heart. She mustn't.

She had to concentrate on Lisa's future—a future away from Gundowring.

She'd have to tell her tonight. . . .

Maybe she should tell her now? The thought flashed through her distressed mind while she read and she shook her head. Time enough for distress when the pain was within reach—when there was only a night to go.

The story was longer than she'd thought—or maybe there was just too much giggling for the reader to concentrate. By the time they'd breakfasted and Gina had showered she was running late. The phone rang as she twisted her hair up into the efficient knot she used for work.

'There's a fisherman in Casualty with a hook in his leg,' the charge nurse told her. 'Can you come?'

'I'm on my way.' Gina dropped a kiss on to Lisa's head, grabbed her white coat, adjusted the door so the children's ward sister could see her two charges and took off down the corridor as swiftly as her stiff leg would let her.

The fisherman's leg was a mess. Fish hooks were usually easy to remove—simply a matter of injecting local anaesthetic, cutting the eye and pulling the hook through. Professional fishermen knew it—but this man was a tourist. He'd been trawling for barracuda with a huge couta hook. He'd hauled in a fish, cut the fish free, and then slipped as the fish writhed on the floor of the boat, driving the bloodied hook into his calf. By attempting to drag the hook out the way it had entered he'd hopelessly entangled barbs in flesh, and he was nauseous with pain.

In the end Gina had to anaesthetise him and cut the hook free. It took a good half an hour to make sure the wound was clean. She stitched the gash, wincing over the ragged scar he'd given himself, and then asked Sister to keep an eye on the patient for an hour or so.

'I'll come back and check in half an hour,' she promised the would-be fisherman. 'But I want you flat on your back until you get some colour back.'

The fisherman didn't object. All the bluster had gone out of him. He sat with his wife gripping his hand hard, and Gina smiled to herself, thinking how much better children handled wounds like this than grown men.

Children. . .

She still hadn't done her ward-rounds but she'd just check on Lisa. This was the last day she'd be able to do so.

Lisa wasn't there.

Gina put her head around the open door and called, but no Lisa popped out to greet her. No puppy either.

Gina looked back to the sister's station in the children's ward. The sister had her head down over hand-over charts.

'Is Lisa outside?' she called, and the sister's head came up.

'She was watching *Playschool* five minutes ago.' The nurse looked over to where Jack Messer was propped up on pillows watching the same programme. 'It's still on. I thought——' She came hurrying down the corridor. 'She likes *Playschool*. Maybe she's just gone to the toilet?'

Gina was already over the partition. She walked forward to the bathroom and flung the door open. 'No.'

'Then, outside?' The nurse frowned. 'I wouldn't have thought. . .' She looked down at the sofa. The television was still on and there was a half-eaten piece of toast on the table. And Sam Tiger. . .

'Lisa?' Gina's voice rose. She threw open the door to the garden. 'Lisa? Wacky?'

She stared out. Nothing. . . Then a high-pitched yap sounded and Wacky came tearing down the path towards her. From the road-gate.

The road-gate. . .

Gina was running, her stiff hip forgotten. Halfway along the path Wacky met her, but she ignored him and kept running. The little dog turned, puzzled, and then trotted back after her.

The road was deserted. It was early morning in Gundowring. The local children had just started school, the shops were hardly open and the fishing fleet was out. Nothing.

No Lisa. . .

'She wouldn't have come out this way,' the nurse faltered. 'Would she?'

Gina frowned. 'I can't imagine. . .' She shook her head, trying to make herself think. 'But Wacky was out here. She must have opened the door for him. So. . .'

'Maybe she's tried to go home?' the nurse suggested.

Without Sam Tiger? 'Maybe. . .' Gina stood, indecisive, with worry mounting. 'I'll check the flat again. Then I guess I'll just have to drive out there. She'll be on the road somewhere.'

'Kids do it all the time,' the nurse said, as though trying to reassure herself. 'We had Ricky Thomas only three weeks ago decide to walk home—on a broken leg.' She smiled apologetically. 'I'll have to go back to the ward.'

'Yes. Of course.' Wacky was whining at her legs and Gina picked him up. The whining didn't stop. It was as if the little dog was worried.

So was Gina. She walked back into the flat and methodically searched. There was always the chance that Lisa had decided to play a game. She checked under beds and at the back of wardrobes, the pup whining at her feet the entire time. One more check, she promised herself, but as she walked into the bedroom the telephone rang.

'Dr Gina Buchanan?'

Gina froze. The colour drained out of her face and she put a hand on the bedside table to steady herself. She knew that voice.

'Y-yes.' Her voice was a fearful whisper.

'You recognise me.' The man sounded smugly satisfied. 'Well, well. I'm glad I made such an impression in our short aquaintance.'

Michael Carter. . . Her worst nightmare.

'What. . .what do you want?'

'You killed my dog.' Smooth, conversational. . . As if discussing the weather.

'I had to.'

'Yeah, well. . .' He sniffed into the phone. 'Two can play at that game, bitch. You killed my dog. I've got your kid.'

Your kid. . .

Lisa.

Her knees sagged, and Gina sank nervelessly on to the bed. The memory of the silhouette on the beach came back. It must have been Carter. He'd seen her with Lisa. He must have assumed. . .

'Don't. . . Don't hurt her.'

'It's going to give me a bloody lot of satisfaction to hurt her,' he said smoothly. 'Unless. . .'

'Unless?'

'Unless you agree to a small proposal I have in mind. I might be prepared to negotiate.'

'What?' She couldn't think of a thing to say. 'What do you want?'

'I want you, sweetheart. I'm in for a long stretch in the slammer, and I know I can't get out of it. A man can't stay on the run forever. I just want. . .' He sighed, a long sound of anticipation. 'I just want it to be worth it.'

'So?'

'So. So be up at the look-out in half an hour. The place where we first met. We get to renew our aquaint-ance. And if you don't show. . . If you don't show then the kid gets what I gave the other interfering b——'

'Don't. . . Please, don't hurt her. Please. . .'

'Then be here. Half an hour. And if one other person shows but you, one cop or anyone else, then the kid dies. I'm in for attempted murder anyway, and with my record the sentence won't be much more if I actu-ally kill. So I've got nothing to lose. Be there.'

'But——'

'Now I'm not going to kill you,' he said softly, so softly that Gina could barely hear the pleasure and anticipation in his voice. It took her a moment to realise he was actually trying to reassure her. 'I wouldn't do that to a broad who looks as good as you—much as you deserve it. All right, you killed my dog, but I can accept payment in lieu. All I want is what I wanted in the first place.'

'Rape?' Gina could hardly make herself whisper.

'Now that's not a nice word, is it, sweetheart? It's not rape when I have your full consent to everything I do. Everything. And if you don't consent—then, yes, I'll be forced to kill. You or the kid. But you wouldn't be so stupid. . .'

'I——'

'That's enough,' he snapped. 'Just get here. Fast. Oh, and, sweetheart. . .'

'Yes?'

'I'll be sitting on the rail overlooking the drop. With the kid beside me. So don't try anything.'

CHAPTER TWELVE

THE phone went dead. The dial-tone went on and on while Gina sat lifelessly and stared at the blank wall by the bed.

Dear God. . .

She'd have to go. She knew enough of Mick to know that it was Lisa's only chance. He'd have no compunction in killing.

Maybe he'd already killed?

She couldn't let herself think that. That was the way of madness. Gina took a deep breath, forcing herself to stand. Forcing herself to think. . . The room was swimming in a nauseating haze.

'Dr Buchanan?'

It was a disembodied voice through the telephone. Gina was still holding the receiver in her hand and a woman's voice was sounding urgently through the receiver. Mechanically, Gina lifted it to her ear.

'Y-yes?'

'It's Maggie from the switchboard.' The girl on the line was breathing heavily, as if she too was terrified. 'I know I'm not supposed to—but the man who just called was rude when he asked to speak to you, so I listened. I heard everything. Do you. . .? Should I call the police?'

'No!' It was an instinctive, fearful reaction. Gina had watched while Michael Carter had tried to murder Lloyd. He'd have no hesitation in killing Lisa at the first sign of a policeman.

'But you can't do what he says. You won't go there!' The girl sucked in her breath in horror. 'You can't. Miss. . . Dr Buchanan, he'll kill you.'

'And if I don't go, then he'll kill Lisa.'

Gina looked down at her watch, her mind not on the conversation. It would take twenty minutes to reach the look-out. She dared not be late.

'Dr Buchanan, I have to tell someone.' Maggie's voice rose on a wail of distress. 'I'm sorry, but I can't sit here while you go to that. . .that. . .'

Gina stared blankly at the wall, willing some answers to be written there. Nothing. . .

Struan. . . If she could contact Struan. . .

Struan knew the local police. He'd know whether they were likely to go in, guns blazing, risking Lisa's life to catch a criminal. He'd know.

She didn't have time to ring him.

'Dr Maitland,' she whispered to Maggie. 'You could tell him.'

The telephonist let her breath out in relief. 'Yeah. . . He'll know. . . I'll try and locate him straight away. I think he might be on a house-call, though.'

'Get him as soon as you can, Maggie. Tell him everything. But I can't wait. Tell him I've gone.'

It took Gina a little more than twenty minutes to reach the look-out. She'd driven her car faster than was safe, but a farmer herding his cows placidly along the road at the foot of the mountain had cost her five nerve-wrenching minutes. By the time she swung the car into the car park by the look-out there were two minutes to go before the stipulated half-hour was up, and Michael Carter was already on the rail by the cliff-drop, looking as if he had nothing better to do than to enjoy the view.

Lisa was with him. She was huddled close. At first sight Carter's arm might have been around Lisa to prevent her falling to the rocks below. Only Gina knew it wasn't.

She stopped the car twenty feet from the drop and

emerged slowly. For the life of her, she didn't know what to do.

'Lisa. . .'

Lisa looked across and gave a whimpering cry. The man's arm tightened.

'You're not going anywhere, kid.' He lifted his free hand and it held a pistol. He pointed it straight at Gina.

A gun. . . She hadn't thought of a gun.

She hadn't thought of anything. Only Lisa.

The child was wide-eyed and bewildered. She stared at Gina with uncomprehending eyes, as though wondering why Gina wasn't whisking her away from this nightmare—away from this unshaved, filthy oaf of a man. And all Gina could do was stare down the barrel of the gun.

'Let her go,' she breathed. 'I've come.'

'So you have.' He eyed her white coat and neat hairstyle with satisfaction. 'So you really are a doctor?'

'I really am a doctor.' She forced her voice to stay calm. 'And you don't want to hurt me, Mick. Or Lisa. We haven't done anything to you.'

'You killed my dog.'

'I know.' Gina spread her hands. 'And I'm sorry. I didn't have a choice, as it happened, but I'm sorry I killed him.'

'I'll bet.' He spat into the dust at his feet, and then looked up and smiled. 'You're going to get a lot sorrier, you know,' he told her. 'Any minute now.'

'You can make me as sorry as you like. Just let Lisa go.'

'Take your coat off.'

'I. . .I beg your pardon?'

'Take it off.' Then, as she stood hesitating before him, he lowered the pistol and fired once into the dust at her feet. The bullet dug deep into the earth, scattering gravel up to sting into her ankles. Gina took an involuntary step back.

'You get any closer to the car and the kid goes backwards.' Mick was in control and revelling in it. 'Take your coat off.'

She had no choice. Gina stared helplessly at the gun, slipped off her coat and let it fall to her feet.

He considered. He was taking his time, sadistic in the humiliation he intended inflicting. 'A nice blouse,' he said at last. 'Take it off.'

'Let Lisa go first.'

For answer he lifted the gun and fired again, this time almost touching her feet with the bullet. Lisa gave a sob and pulled away, but he wrenched her back.

'The blouse, bitch. And the next time I have to repeat a request, I'll fire straight at your ankles. You can still do what I want with your ankles broken.'

Gina looked at Lisa and the child's eyes held hers— terrified, but at the same time trusting. Whatever awful things were being threatened, Lisa still believed that somehow Gina would get them out of it.

Struan. . . Had Maggie reached Struan?

There was nothing Struan could do anyway. There was only Gina between Lisa and this man—and she was useless. Slowly, slowly, playing for as much time as she could, Gina unbuttoned her blouse and let it fall the same way as her coat. She stood in her serviceable skirt, respectable from the waist down, with only a flimsy wisp of white lace covering her breasts.

'Very nice.' Mick gave a grunt of satisfaction. 'What do you reckon next? Not a lot of choice, really. I reckon the bra. Now, lady!'

Gina closed her eyes. This was almost rape in slow motion. That he should make her do this—and in front of Lisa.

She put her hand to the small of her back to undo the clasp, and then froze. A shout, a savage oath, and Mick was tumbling backwards off the rail, falling towards the drop. And Lisa was still in his grasp.

There was someone dragging Mick backwards. She heard a vicious curse, a shot and an oath of pain. Gina hardly registered who was doing the shouting. All she saw was Lisa, fighting to keep her balance as Mick's encircling arm hauled her back.

She launched herself in a flying leap towards the child. She had never moved so fast in all her life as Lisa swayed and Mick's arms released her. Mick was fighting to fend off the arms grabbing him from below, but Gina's only thought was Lisa.

Somehow she reached her. . .somehow before Lisa's slight body had a chance to topple backwards. Then she had the child in her arms, dragging her forward to safety, cradling her against her half-naked body and sobbing in fear and confusion.

Struan. . .

He was there. She could see the top of his head, unmistakable with the jet-black hair. He was somehow balanced on a ledge just below the rail—and he was hauling Mick backwards, down to him. There was someone else—a blue uniform and a raised arm with black service pistol. . .

Another gun-shot, making Gina flinch with horror and hold the child closer. She couldn't see what was happening—the men were below the level of the ledge—half fighting for control of the guns, and fighting also to keep their footing on the precarious ledge.

'Give it up.' Struan's voice raised in savage urgency. 'For God's sake, man, drop the gun. You don't have a——'

His words were cut off as if something had hit him hard. A raised hand above the ledge. . . It could have been anyone's. Gina couldn't see, and she had the child. The pistol rang out once again—whose?

An oath of pain—Struan?—and then a man's scream of blind terror. A thump against rock—an oath—and then the cry went on. Over, down, down, and then nothing.

Dear God. . .

She didn't dare go to the cliff-edge. She didn't dare look. She had the child in her arms and Mick had a gun. Gina turned away from the edge, stiff with fear, and knelt to cradle the child to her.

There was a long, long silence. Then there was a scrambling of feet down the rough cliff—voices, but she couldn't hear whose. All she knew was that Lisa was rigid with terror and her place—for now—was with Lisa. Whatever was happening.

'It's OK, Lisa. It's all over.' Please God, it was. Please. . .

A hand came down on her shoulder. She jerked in fright and looked up, but it wasn't Carter. A kindly, middle-aged face was watching her with concern.

She'd met this man before. His blue uniform denoted just who he was.

'Are you all right, Doc?' he was asking.

'Yes.' Somehow she managed to get the word out, though what she realy wanted to say wouldn't come.

'And the kiddy?'

'Lisa?' Gina swallowed and put the child a little out from her, so she could see the tear-ravaged face. 'Did he hurt you?'

'I'm OK,' Lisa said bravely. 'He was nasty, but he said you'd come, Gina, and you did.' She put her arms around Gina's neck and burst into tears.

Silence. Why wouldn't the policeman say something? Finally she forced the word into her mouth.

'Struan. . .'

'He'll be up in a minute.'

'He's——?' Her eyes flashed up disbelievingly. 'He's alive? The gun-shots. . .?'

'He's OK,' the policeman said grimly. 'A graze to his arm, but he'll live. Which is more than can be said for the other one.' He looked down at Lisa, and decided she was past shocking. 'Broke his neck. Doc Maitland's just checking. He reckoned he had to go down, but the angle he was lying at—well, I don't reckon there's any chance at all. Sent me up to you.'

'But if Mick's still alive. . .' Gina's breath drew in in fear. 'Go back. . . Please. . .' she managed, but there was no need.

Struan was coming. She could hear him below the cliff.

There were swift, urgent footsteps across the gravel, and Struan was there. He knelt before her and took woman and child into his bloodstained arms.

'My Gina,' he whispered as he gathered them close. 'My heart.'

Later—much later—when ambulance officers were down the cliff-face retrieving what remained of Michael Carter and police officers were measuring and taping off sections of the cliff-top for forensic examination, Gina finally discovered what had happened.

'Believe it or not, I was trying to stop him falling when he shot me,' Struan told her.

They were sitting a little way from the cliff-edge, letting the morning sun restore warmth and promise of a world after this nightmare. Struan's arm was bandaged where one of Carter's shots had grazed him. 'If he hadn't shot me he'd be alive now.'

'But you pulled him off the ledge.'

'We reckoned it was our only chance,' Struan explained.

His good arm was holding her tight, and Lisa was cradled between them. One of the ambulance officers had offered to take her, but Lisa had clung closer. She was where she needed to be.

'We could have shot him from behind—he was so busy watching you—but Lisa was too darned close for

comfort, and we thought if we overbalanced him. . .'
He shook his head. 'Then, when he fired that last shot,
I just lost my head. I couldn't see what he was shooting.
I hauled him off without waiting for Bob to catch up.
We'd figured on grabbing an arm each, but I stuffed
it up—gave him a chance to shoot.'

'You didn't stuff anything up,' Gina whispered. 'You
came.' She shook her head. 'How. . .? How did
you. . .?'

He pulled her closer and landed a light kiss on her
hair. 'When Maggie rang I went straight to the police—
I knew Bob wouldn't make a botch of it. We decided
if we came up the road we risked him killing you. The
road to the look-out is circuitous, though. By taking
the motorbike to the foot of the cliff and climbing we
reckoned we could reach here almost the same time
you did. There's thick bush below, and a main road
not far off. He wouldn't see the bike and he wouldn't
be able to differentiate the noise of the bike from
normal traffic.'

'So we owe our reprieve to the Harley Davidson,'
Gina grimaced. 'I don't believe it.'

He smiled down at her. 'Does this mean I might be
able to marry you and keep the bike?

'Oh, Struan. . .' Gina looked up at his caring, smiling eyes. There was love there. After all she had
done. . . He'd risked everything for her.

He'd lost once before but he'd had the courage to
start again. He had the courage to love.

She had called him dangerous. Not dangerous. Brave
and wonderful and beloved. . .

How could she not put her heart in his hands?

'I'll marry you with anything you like,' she whispered. 'I don't even mind if you grow the beard back.'

His eyes blazed with sudden triumph. His arms held
her closer. 'Not likely,' he said.

'Why. . .? Why not?'

'Because it would keep you a fraction further away from me,' he told her, his eyes loving her. 'And I intend to stay as close as I can—for the rest of my life.'

As close as he could. . .

Lisa stirred slightly within their combined hold, and looked up at Gina. 'I think he wants to be your daddy,' she announced.

Gina smiled as Struan reached out to hug the child. 'Daddy sounds good.' Struan grinned. 'Every respectable family should have at least one. Daddy, Mummy, child and dog. A whole family in the making. What say you, Dr Buchanan? Do you have the courage to pick up the pieces and put them together? As a family?'

Gina's eyes filled with tears. Her love was swirling before her in a mist of happiness.

'A family,' she whispered. 'I haven't had a family for so long. . .I can't think of anything I want more.'

He kissed her then, and the rest of her reply was left as a song in her heart. A song that would echo forever.

Especially if it starts with you.

Look for Lloyd's own story next month, in
ENCHANTING SURGEON,
when surgeon Sally Atchinson makes a real
difference in his life. . .

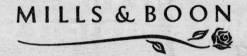

MILLS & BOON

LOVE CALL

The books for enjoyment this month are:

NEVER SAY NEVER	Margaret Barker
DANGEROUS PHYSICIAN	Marion Lennox
THE CALL OF DUTY	Jessica Matthews
FLIGHT INTO LOVE	Meredith Webber

Treats in store!

Watch next month for the following absorbing stories:

A FAMILIAR STRANGER	Caroline Anderson
ENCHANTING SURGEON	Marion Lennox
DOWNLAND CLINIC	Margaret O'Neill
A MATTER OF ETHICS	Patricia Robertson

Available from W.H. Smith, John Menzies, Forbuoys, Martins, Tesco, Asda, Safeway and other paperback stockists.

Readers in South Africa - write to:
IBS, Private Bag X3010, Randburg 2125.

GET 4 BOOKS
AND A MYSTERY GIFT

Return this coupon and we'll send you 4 Love on Call novels and a mystery gift absolutely FREE! We'll even pay the postage and packing for you.

We're making you this offer to introduce you to the benefits of Reader Service: FREE home delivery of brand-new Love on Call novels, at least a month before they are available in the shops, FREE gifts and a monthly Newsletter packed with information.

Accepting these FREE books and gift places you under no obligation to buy, you may cancel at any time, even after receiving just your free shipment. Simply complete the coupon below and send it to:

MILLS & BOON READER SERVICE, FREEPOST, CROYDON, SURREY, CR9 3WZ.

No stamp needed

Yes, please send me 4 free Love on Call novels and a mystery gift. I understand that unless you hear from me, I will receive 4 superb new titles every month for just £1.99* each postage and packing free. I am under no obligation to purchase any books and I may cancel or suspend my subscription at any time, but the free books and gifts will be mine to keep in any case. (I am over 18 years of age)

2EP5D

Ms/Mrs/Miss/Mr _____

Address _____

_____

_____ Postcode _____

Offer closes 31st March 1996. We reserve the right to refuse an application. *Prices and terms subject to change without notice. Offer only valid in UK and Ireland and is not available to current subscribers to this series. **Readers in Ireland please write to: P.O. Box 4546, Dublin 24.** Overseas readers please write for details.

You may be mailed with offers from other reputable companies as a result of this application. Please tick box if you would prefer not to receive such offers. ☐

MILLS & BOON

Betty Neels

Bestselling romances brought back to you by popular demand

Two complete novels in one volume
by bestselling author

Betty Neels

The Convenient Wife
Roses Have Thorns

Available: October 1995   Price: £3.99

*Available from WH Smith, John Menzies, Forbuoys, Martins,
Tesco, Asda, Safeway and other paperback stockists.*